SPACE TAXI

4 BOOKS IN 1!

ARCHIE TAKES FLIGHT

WATER PLANET RESCUE

ARCHIE'S ALIEN DISGUISE

THE GALACTIC B.U.R.P.

By Wendy Mass and Michael Brawer

Illustrated by Elise Gravel and Keith Frawley

Ⓛ Ⓑ

LITTLE, BROWN AND COMPANY

New York   Boston

Copyright © 2014, 2015, 2016 by Wendy Mass and Michael Brawer
Illustrations from *Space Taxi: Archie Takes Flight* and *Space Taxi: Water Planet Rescue* copyright © 2014 by Elise Gravel
Illustrations from *Space Taxi: Archie's Alien Disguise* and *Space Taxi: The Galactic B.U.R.P.* by Keith Frawley, based on the art of Elise Gravel

Little, Brown and Company

Hachette Book Group
1290 Avenue of the Americas, New York, NY 10104
Visit us at lb-kids.com

Little, Brown and Company is a division of Hachette Book Group, Inc.
The Little, Brown name and logo are trademarks of Hachette Book Group, Inc.

The publisher is not responsible for websites (or their content) that are not owned by the publisher.

First Bindup Edition: May 2016
Space Taxi: Archie Takes Flight first published in April 2014 by Little, Brown and Company
Space Taxi: Water Planet Rescue first published in September 2014 by Little, Brown and Company
Space Taxi: Archie's Alien Disguise first published in April 2015 by Little, Brown and Company
Space Taxi: The Galactic B.U.R.P. first published in May 2016 by Little, Brown and Company

ISBN 978-0-316-35789-0

10 9 8 7 6 5 4 3 2 1

RRD-C

Printed in the United States of America

SPACE TAXI

ARCHiE TAKES FLiGHT

By Wendy Mass and Michael Brawer

Illustrated by Elise Gravel

Ⓛ Ⓑ
LITTLE, BROWN AND COMPANY
New York   Boston

To our favorite copilots,
Griffin and Chloe

CONTENTS

Chapter One:

Take Your Kid to Work Day

Beep! Beep! Beep! Beep!

It's not every day a regular kid like me gets to wake up at midnight. But this is no regular day. Today is Take Your Kid to Work Day, and I'm going to ride with Dad in his taxi! Dad works the night shift, so he's usually awake when I'm asleep and asleep when I'm awake. But not tonight.

I've been waiting eight years, eight months, and eight days for this day to arrive. Instead of staring at the maps of the big city taped to my walls, I'll actually get to go places. Mom likes to keep us close to home, but I'm itching to explore. My little sister, Penny, is the same way. Any open door and she takes off like she's late for something important.

Mom sticks her head in my room. "Archie Morningstar, aren't you up yet? Dad's waiting outside."

Mom always uses my full name when she wants to make sure I'm paying attention. I wish I had a normal last name that no one would tease me about. The *real*

Morning Star is a nickname for the planet Venus, which is so bright you can still see it as the sun rises. Maybe Morningstar would be a cool name if I lived in the country and could actually *see* the stars and planets. But here in the city all we can see is bright lights and smog.

I jump out of bed, fully dressed.

She frowns. "Did you even sleep at all? It's going to be a long night and you don't want to fall asleep on the job."

I shake my head. "I was too excited to sleep. But I'm not tired, I promise." I hurry over to the window. Dad's yellow taxi gleams under the streetlight. He keeps it really clean, even though it's old and clunky and most mornings he comes home without any hubcaps on his tires.

I push up my window. "I'm coming, Dad!"

Mom groans. "Archie, it's midnight. You probably woke your sister. And half the block."

"Oops, sorry." I run over to my desk and grab the one thing I don't go anywhere without—the metal tube my grandpa gave me before he retired to Florida. It looks kind of like an empty paper-towel roll, but it's black with a single silver star painted on it. I bring it with me to baseball practice, to school, even to the bathroom! My friends are so used to seeing it they don't even tease me anymore. Well, not much, anyway. When Grandpa gave it to me, he told me I'd need it one day and I'd know when that day arrived. So until that day comes, it goes where I go. "See ya later, Mom!"

"Archie, wait," she says.

I stop, pretty sure she's going to tell me to leave the tube at home, like she always does.

But Mom doesn't mention the tube. Instead, she hands me a brown bag and a warm thermos. It's the same thing she gives Dad before he leaves every night. It would be dorky to show how cool I think this is, so I just take it and mumble, "Thanks."

"Let me take one last look at you," she says, wiping her eyes. "I never thought this day would come. I'm going to miss you."

Mom can be so mushy, always hugging and smooching me. She doesn't like it when

I complain that I'm too old for that stuff. So I hold in my groan and say, "Oh, Mom. I'm only going to the other side of town."

"Well...it may be a little farther than that, honey." She pulls me in for a hug.

"I'll be fine," I tell her, squirming away after what I feel is a reasonable period of time. "I'll be with Dad."

She opens her mouth to say something, but instead she kisses me on the cheek, whispers, "I love you, honey," and shuts the door behind me.

Chapter Two:
Barney's Bagels and Schmear

With my supplies in hand, the dark night before me, and Mom inside, I'm feeling pretty grown up right about now. I hold up my thermos and paper bag. "Hi, Dad, I'm ready to go to work!"

He lets out a deep, rumbly laugh.

"Buckle up then, Archie! You're in for a wild ride."

I carefully place Grandpa's tube on the floor behind my seat and put my seat belt on. The old taxi rattles and groans as we pull away from the curb. I don't think the ride's going to get too wild. Our biggest adventure will probably be going over a bump and losing a hubcap!

I've never heard the streets so quiet. It's almost spooky. I shiver, even though it's not cold. I have to remember not to let my imagination run away with me. That's what Mom used to tell me when I was a little kid and thought a four-armed, three-eyed alien was living under the kitchen sink. Plus, I'll be with Dad, and he does this every night.

I look around at the empty streets. "How do you find someone who needs a ride?" I ask.

"I get my assignments from the depot," Dad explains. "Then I go pick up my fare. That's what we call the person—or people—who need a ride. Then I take them wherever they want to go. It's different every night. And tonight I'll have my best pal along for the ride. Sounds like an adventure, right?"

Feeling better, I smile back at him. "Right, Dad!"

A few minutes later we pull up in front of Barney's Bagels and Schmear. It's not closed for the night like the rest of the restaurants and stores in the area. Through the large window I can see that half the tables are full with people eating, sipping coffee, talking, and laughing.

"Our first stop," Dad says, turning off the car.

"But Mom already gave us food," I say, pointing to the brown bag at my feet.

"That's breakfast," he says with a grin. "This is a midnight snack."

As Dad pushes the door open, all the eyes in the place look up. Some people shout, "Hey, Morningstar, how's it going?" Others wave or give the thumbs-up sign. Dad shouts back greetings and leads me to the counter. For a second I think I see what looks like a dog wearing headphones slip out the back door. I rub my eyes. Mom was right. I probably should have gotten some sleep.

Dad orders us each a tuna sandwich on a bagel, along with a coffee for him and an apple juice for me.

"Is this your boy?" the man asks as he neatly slices our poppy-seed bagels. He has a big, round belly and a happy smile.

Dad nods and pats me on the shoulder. "This is Archie. He's eight years, eight months, and eight days old today."

"Big day for you, eh, young Morningstar?" the man says, and then winks. At least I think he winked. Maybe a poppy seed flew into his eye.

I almost tell him that it's a big *night* for me, not day, but Mom always says it's rude to correct people. So I just nod and say, "I've never seen the city at night before."

"You're gonna see a lot more than that," he says, winking again. Those poppy seeds must really fly! Someone behind us chuckles and I turn around. For a split second it looks like a lady sitting at the counter has one more head than she's supposed to have. But when I blink again, she goes back to normal.

Okay, I *definitely* see a nap happening in my near future.

On the way out of the deli, Dad stops at almost every table. How does he know all these people? When we get to the street, I ask, "Are we going to the depot now?"

"We just did," he replies, pulling a slip of paper from the bag holding the sandwiches.

"Huh?" I look behind us at the bagel shop. All the customers are crowded by the window, watching us. When they see me looking, they quickly run back to their seats. Life after midnight is weird.

"Let's go, son." Dad steers me toward

the car. He hands me the piece of paper and says, "Our first pickup awaits."

I read the handwritten words:

Mr. Ramsey Fitch
751 Zoder Street,
Apartment C
Delta Three, South Quadrant,
Cygnus Galaxy

Not to brag, but I'm pretty familiar with the city. I've memorized all the maps on my walls. I've never seen any South Quadrant, Cygnus Galaxy. When we're both in the car, I ask, "Is this on the other side of the city, Dad?"

He smiles. "It may be a little farther."

My eyes widen. "You mean like the next town over?"

He smiles again and pats my knee. "Something like that."

I buckle up in a hurry. Forget the nap—I'm way too excited now. A midnight visit to the next town over. Wait till the kids at school hear about this!

Chapter Three:
The Next Town Over

The car starts with its usual clanging and banging. Once we're on the road, I ask, "Hey, Dad, how do you know all those people in the bagel place?"

"Oh, I've known them for years," he says, adjusting his rearview mirror. "Most of them are drivers, like me. Some are copilots."

"Copilots? Taxi drivers have copilots?"

He laughs. "Of course. We'd get hopelessly lost without them."

"But *you* don't have one."

"I used to. Yesterday was his last day."

"Huh? But you never—" Suddenly the dashboard lights up in a rainbow of colors. Buttons, knobs, and screens pop out of the flat surface. My eyes bug out of my head. That definitely did *not* happen on the way to the restaurant!

Dad reaches for a knob marked COM LINE and twists it two notches to the left. "Sal Morningstar reporting for duty."

"Good evening, Morningstar," a squeaky voice crackles through the car. "This is

Home Base. Do you have the instructions for your first pickup?"

"Affirmative. I'm heading to the field now."

Field? What field? The only field I know of in the city is the one I play Little League baseball on, and we already passed it.

"Be careful out there," the voice warns. It sounds like a mouse in a cartoon.

"Always am," Dad replies. "Morningstar out." He turns the knob back again without even looking.

"What was *that* about, Dad? What's a com line?"

"That's how I communicate with Home Base," he replies, veering the car hard to the left.

"What's Home Base?" I twist around in

my seat and look behind us. Where did the city go? It's so dark. "Where are we?"

"Hold on, Archie!" We whiz past a sign that says AIRFIELD.

"Um, Dad?" I grip the sides of my seat with all my strength. "Aren't airfields where planes take off?"

"Yup!" Dad says. Before I can even form my next thought, a second seat belt reaches across my body and pins me tightly to the back of the seat.

The car grunts, and even in the darkness I can tell it's changing. The hood stretches out until it's much longer and rounder. The roof grows higher above our heads. "Dad! Are those... *WINGS*?" I have to shout over the sound of the engine, which is getting louder with every second.

A keypad swooshes out from the dashboard, and Dad's right hand flies over the keys.

"Dad!" I shout. "Can you please tell me what's going on? I thought you were a taxi driver!"

"I am, son. Now, this is gonna feel a bit strange, but trust me, you're totally safe."

I tighten my grip on the arms of my seat. Dad presses a red button and... *BANG! BOOM! KA-BLAMO!*

Fire explodes from the back of the car. We zoom down a runway that I didn't even see in the dark. All four hubcaps fly off and spin in different directions. We're going so fast I don't even hear them land. And then, before I can catch my breath, we're going UP! Straight UP! Into the SKY!

I want to ask Dad if I'm dreaming, but

I can't seem to make words come out of my mouth. My heart is thumping so loudly I bet Mom can hear it back home.

Mom!

She would FREAK OUT if she knew about this! If I ever make it home again, she can hug me as long as she wants. Seriously. And I won't complain about the kisses, either. I'll even take 'em from Penny, and hers usually leave a smear of peanut butter on my cheek.

My jaw drops as we pass the moon.

THE MOON!

I've never been on an airplane before, but I'm pretty sure we're not supposed to be this high.

Dad's talking and pointing out the window, but I can't focus on a word he says. He pulls a lever below the steering

23

wheel and we slow down a little. I finally remember to breathe. We are still moving really, REALLY fast, though.

I begin to notice the stars. Lots and lots of stars. More stars than I ever imagined existed. I stare and stare. I can't see the moon anymore. Is that…*Saturn*? We swerve to the right to avoid what looks like a giant chunk of ice, then bank to the left.

It's a good thing we haven't eaten those tuna sandwiches yet. Mine would be splattered all over the windshield by now.

"Here, Archie," Dad says, handing me a rolled-up paper scroll.

I stare at him. He *looks* like my dad. He *sounds* like my dad. But we're in OUTER SPACE and he doesn't seem NEARLY as surprised as he should be.

"It's a map," he explains, pointing to the

scroll clutched in my hand. "I'll need you to tell me when we reach the third wormhole. They're invisible, of course."

I want to shout, "THERE ARE GIANT WORMS MAKING HOLES IN OUTER SPACE AND YOU WANT ME TO *FIND* ONE? On *PURPOSE*?" But I'm still too shocked to speak. I unroll the paper and spread it out on my lap. This is not easy because my hands won't stop shaking.

The map isn't like any I've ever seen. Thick green lines crisscross each other, dotted here and there with red and blue splotches, and in the center is one small yellow circle. Tiny numbers are printed along each line in some sort of pattern. "Um, Dad? I have no idea what I'm looking at." My voice comes out weird, like a croaking frog. A really freaked-out croaking frog.

"You can do this, son. Just give it a try."

"But I don't—"

He pats my knee. "You'll figure it out. I *should* mention, though, if we miss the wormhole, I'll be late for my pickup. And late getting you back home. And then we'll both have to deal with your mother."

I stare at him, then back at the map. This is crazy. Why would Dad think I could see something that's invisible? I stare hard at the paper, but all I see are those lines and numbers and dots.

And then...*BAM!* Right in front of my eyes it changes. The images on the map rise off the paper and I'm staring at a 3-D image of outer space. It's hovering right there over my lap! The small yellow circle is now a perfect image of our taxi! Is

that...yes! I can see me and Dad inside, zooming through space.

The images of the planets and stars are so real I almost feel like I can reach out and touch them. So I do! As soon as my finger lands on one of the glowing spheres, the air around the object fills with information. I touch a wormhole (which, invisible or not, I can clearly see), and words pop up to tell me that a wormhole is a tunnel connecting two distant points in space.

I look at Dad in amazement. "How does this...what...why...?" I can't seem to make the words come out right.

Dad laughs. "You see it now, don't you?"

"I see...everything! The whole universe, I think."

"It must be quite amazing."

"Can't you see it, too?" I ask, surprised.

He shakes his head.

"Why not?" I ask.

"I'll explain later," he says, speeding up again. "Right now I need you to guide me to the third wormhole. Make sure it's the third, and not the fourth."

My heart thumps loudly again as I try to sort out the different wormholes. They all look the same. "What happens if I choose the fourth by mistake?"

Dad shudders. "Let's hope we never find out."

Chapter Four:
The Trip

"Turn right!" I shout. "Now, Dad!"

Dad yanks the wheel and shouts, "Yee-ha!"

We plunge into the wormhole, and the night takes on a whole new level of strange. The stars disappear like someone turned off a huge switch in the sky. Streaks of color fly past our windows almost faster than I can see them. I gasp as we twist and turn like we're on the universe's longest roller coaster. I think I'm going to be sick.

On the plus side, no real worms.

The whole time we're on this crazy ride, Dad is leaning back in his seat, grinning wildly. He looks like a kid who just found out he's going to Disney World instead of the dentist's office.

"I knew you could do it, Archie!" Dad says, beaming at me. "The day you were born, your grandpa bet you'd be an even greater space map reader than him. And he was one of the best!"

I try to answer, but the car plunges into

a series of loop-de-loops. I clamp my lips and eyes shut.

"It'll straighten out in a few seconds," Dad promises as the car flips upside down for the third time.

They are a few LONG seconds, but finally we stop looping and enter an area of gentle curves. I open my eyes and take a few deep breaths before saying, "Grandpa was a *space map reader*? But he sold hats for a living."

Dad shakes his head. "And he didn't retire to Florida, either. He's currently tanning himself on a planet where one of three suns is always shining."

"There's a planet with three suns?"

Dad spreads his arms wide. "You wouldn't BELIEVE the kinds of planets there are. The universe is an amazing place, Archie. I'm so glad you're finally getting to see it."

The map on my lap flattens with a faint *whomp*. All the spinning planets and fiery stars have become simple lines and dots again.

"Um, Dad?" I ask. "Are you sure I'm not dreaming all this?"

He shakes his head. "Nope. All real."

"But...all these years, why did you tell me you drove a taxi?"

"I *do* drive a taxi," he says. "It just happens to be a *space* taxi." He leans over and pats the dashboard. "Top of the line, I might add. It only clunks and groans to blend in with regular taxis on Earth."

I stare at him as he keeps talking.

"Our family has been in the space taxi business for five generations," he says. "I'm a driver. I can take my fares anywhere in the universe and still get home in time for breakfast." He clasps me on the shoulder. "And you're a copilot, Archie! Being able to read a space map is a very special talent that runs in families. My father had it, so I'd hoped you'd get it, but I didn't know for sure until today—when you turned eight years, eight months, and eight days old!"

I shake my head. It all sounds too crazy. "But, Dad, what if choosing this wormhole was just a lucky guess? Maybe we're really in the fourth one, or the second."

He shakes his head. "Trust me, we'd know by now. You're a copilot, all right."

I narrow my eyes at him. "Does Mom know about this?"

Dad laughs. "Of course. You know how hard it is to hide things from your mother."

It's true. Mom can tell if one jelly bean is missing out of a whole bowl. And she always knows *I'm* the one who took it.

"Look," Dad says, pointing ahead of us. I can see two tiny dots of light far in the distance. As we get closer, they grow bigger and bigger. The dashboard springs to life again in a flash of color and sound. Dad takes hold of the wheel.

"We'll need the map," he says. "We're nearing the orbit of Delta Three."

"There's a planet out there?" I ask, seeing nothing planetlike at all.

"Yup. And we're approaching its two suns." Dad hands me a pair of sunglasses and I put them on just in time. We fly out of the wormhole and zip between two *huge* balls of bright yellowish-red flame. For a few seconds the air in the taxi grows superhot, before returning to normal.

At that moment the high-pitched, squeaky voice crackles through the car again. I jump in my seat, surprised anything could still startle me.

"Morningstar, this is Home Base. Please report your current location."

Dad turns the com line knob on. "We're on approach to our pickup on Delta Three."

"Phew!" The voice sighs. "You made it into the right wormhole!"

"Sure did. Thanks to my son, the copilot!"

"Congratulations, young Morningstar," the voice says.

I smile weakly, still not totally convinced

it wasn't beginner's luck. The map in my lap pops up again. I focus in on the tiny image of the yellow taxi hovering above my knee. It's heading right toward a blue-green planet the size of a marble. I look out the windshield. Right in front of us is also a blue-green planet, but it's MUCH bigger than a marble. This must be Delta Three. If it weren't for the two suns, I'd think we were looking down at Earth. This is what the globe in my classroom looks like.

"What do I do, Dad?"

"I'll need you to tell me when we're about to enter the upper atmosphere. It should be around fifteen miles from the planet. Then I'll reverse the thrusters to slow us down. Sound good?"

"Um, sure," I say, not sure at all. I know

from school that the atmosphere surrounds a planet and protects it from the sun and maybe other stuff, but that doesn't mean I know what it looks like.

"And, Archie, I probably don't need to tell you this, but if I don't slow us down in time, well..." He trails off, but I get his message loud and clear.

I gulp and touch the image of the little yellow taxi floating above the map. Lines instantly shoot out of it, with numbers running above them. I quickly realize the numbers are showing me how far we are from the objects around us. The closest is Delta Three, at only forty miles. I breathe a sigh of relief. Archie Morningstar, World's Best Space Taxi Copilot, has done it again. "Reverse thrusters on the count of three... two... one... now!" I shout.

The number on the map changes to fifteen miles. Dad grabs a red handle above his head and pulls it all the way down. The engine grinds and whirs and the taxi shakes, but we don't seem to be losing any speed. The planet is getting closer and bigger by the second. I push my back into the seat, and my hands clamp down on the armrests. Did I mess up? Maybe the numbers mean something else? Maybe they mean how many feet away we are, not miles?

Just when the planet seems close enough to reach out and touch, the front of the taxi tilts up, and we finally slow down. Instead of flying headfirst toward the ground, we're now flying parallel to it, so that's a lot less scary. A loud rumbling sound fills the car.

"Landing gear," Dad explains before I can ask.

We weave past buildings (all painted pink for some reason) and houses (also pink) and trees (still green) until we circle above a landing field that looks just like the one on Earth. For a split second I wonder if Dad's been playing some crazy trick on me and we're actually back home. "Morningstar and son, coming in for a landing," Dad says, and sets us down so gently I don't realize we're on the ground until he says it.

We roll to a stop at the end of a runway. The car shudders back to its original taxi-like state, and Dad drives us out to the road. I had expected aliens to have green skin and tentacles, or maybe scales and five legs. But the people we pass on the street look human, only everyone is really tall, with short hair and long arms and legs, and they kind of glide when they walk.

They must have some really good basketball games here.

A few minutes later we pull up in front of an ordinary-looking apartment building, not much different from our own. Besides the pinkness, I mean.

Dad turns off the car, which gives one last sputter and clunk before going quiet. "We're here!" he says with a grin. "Your first visit to another planet!" As though he's reading my mind, he says, "I know it looks a lot like home. Planets need to follow the same sort of rules in order for life to exist. Wait till you see the Gamma Quadrant, though. Man, the planets in those galaxies are downright weird!"

I grin. "Does that mean you'll take me to work again someday?"

He laughs and undoes his straps. "Let's

42

get through today first, and then we'll see. Ready?"

I nod. I'm about to step onto another planet! I take a deep breath, step out of the car, and instantly begin rising up into the air.

I repeat, I AM FLOATING IN THE AIR. Like a BALLOON! Soon I'm almost as high as the trees lining the street. I should be freaking out, but once you've loop-de-looped through a wormhole and almost plunged headfirst into a planet, this doesn't seem so scary.

Still, a little warning might have been nice.

Chapter Five:
The Fare

Dad freaks out enough for both of us. "Archie!" he yells, running around underneath me. "Grab on to a branch! Quick, before you get higher than the trees!"

I reach out with both arms and legs until I'm able to grab the top branch of the closest tree. The trees on this planet are very tall, much taller than on Earth. I wrap myself around the trunk and hold tight. The suns are pretty bright up here, but luckily I still have my sunglasses on.

"Great job, Archie!" Dad calls, running over to my tree. "Can you climb down?"

I nod. The bark is kind of rough, but when I loosen my grip, I can feel myself start to float again. So I hang on tight and begin climbing down. Around halfway to the ground I'm feeling pretty good about my climbing abilities. A city kid like me doesn't get many chances to climb trees. I should go to the park more often.

"That's it, Archie," Dad calls up. "Keep going."

Still gripping tight with my hands

and feet, I lower myself one more branch. *Whoa!* I suck in my breath. Six inches away from my face is a large white ball of fur. The ball of fur's belly is rising and falling with each breath. I don't dare move. Who knows what a space animal could do to a kid? Drag me back to its cave? Swallow me in one gulp?

The branch creaks. I wince as the creature lifts his head and looks right at me. He has long whiskers, triangle-shaped ears, and bright green eyes.

"Meow," he says, lazily cleaning a paw with his tongue. As he rolls to the side, I can see a few gray patches of fur on his belly. I had been afraid of a cat! A cat that pretty much looks exactly like a cat from Earth. Bigger and fluffier, but not a scary

eat-my-brains-for-breakfast kind of alien by any means.

I inch closer. The cat swishes his tail but doesn't back away. His tail has an odd green circle around the tip, like someone drew a ring around it with a green marker. He isn't wearing a collar, so I can't tell if he belongs to anyone. Holding on tight to the tree with one hand, I reach out the other so he can sniff it. He must not think I'm much of a threat because he lowers his head and lets me pet him. "How'd you get stuck in this tree?" I murmur as I scratch under his neck. He just purrs happily. Cats have always liked me. I should ask for one as a pet.

"How's it coming, Archie?" Dad calls up between the branches.

I say a fast good-bye to the cat and keep scrambling down the tree.

Once I get low enough, Dad grabs me and lowers me to the ground. I'm *finally* standing on another planet! Pushing down gently, but firmly, on the top of my head to keep me from lifting off again, Dad stuffs what look like yellow marbles into each of my pockets. I can feel them tugging me toward the ground.

"Sorry, son," he says, lifting his hand from my head. "I forgot to give you these gravity balls before we left the car. On Earth each of those would weigh a hundred pounds. You'll need them to stay on the ground. There is slightly less gravity here."

"I think I just found that out."

He laughs. "Indeed you did! Now let's

go pick up Mr. Fitch. We're a little behind schedule."

I'm sure it's my fault that Dad's late. What if his fare is really mad? What if my trouble figuring out the map gets Dad fired?

But when we ring the bell, a man with tan skin and very white teeth opens the door with a smile and a cheerful *"Good day!"* I wonder if this is Mr. Fitch. He doesn't look like the other people we've passed. This guy is large. Like, superlarge. Like, pro-wrestler large. The business suit he's wearing looks like it's about to split wide open.

"Are you ready, sir?" my dad asks.

Mr. Fitch nods and steps out onto the porch beside us. He's carrying a long coat in one hand and a brown briefcase in the other. Except for his size, he could be any regular businessman from Earth. He whistles as he follows us out to the taxi.

"Mr. Fitch?" I ask. "There's a cat stuck up a tree. Is he yours?"

Mr. Fitch stops walking. His smile vanishes. "A cat?" he asks. "I'm allergic to cats. You saw one?"

I nod and point up at the tree. "On that branch. He was white, mostly."

Mr. Fitch reaches up and pushes aside the leaves, but the branch is empty.

"We'd better go, sir," Dad says. "I don't want you to be late for your meeting."

Mr. Fitch takes one more peek into the tree, then shrugs. His smile reappears. "If it was there, it's gone now."

Mr. Fitch is so wide he fills up nearly

all of the backseat. Dad calls Home Base on the com line and tells them we're on our way to the drop-off.

Zooming into outer space is easier once you've done it already. Dad explains that Mr. Fitch's business meeting is on Delta Nine, which is in this same solar system, so we won't need the wormhole. He leans over and presses a small blue button in front of me. A keypad springs out of the dashboard. "All you have to do this time, Archie, is map out the most direct route, then program it in with the keypad."

"No problem," I tell him, trying to sound confident so Mr. Fitch won't know I've never done this before. I lean over the map and whisper, "Map, show me Delta Nine." And just like that, the map springs to life. I can see not only Delta Nine but the whole route between it and us. I hadn't really expected that to work!

Apparently, we will have to avoid two solar storms, three asteroid belts, and what looks like a bus full of tourists, but other than that, it's a straight shot. I use the keypad to type in the quickest and safest route. I'm amazed that I can do what I'm doing. I bet I totally ace my next math test.

"Can't we go any faster?" Mr. Fitch asks. His smile is fully gone now. He sneezes three times in a row, blows his nose loudly, then he sneezes some more.

Uh-oh, I must be the reason he's sneezing! I slowly slide down in my seat. Hopefully he won't notice I have a few stray cat hairs on me. I look down at my pants. Okay, more than a few. I pull off one particularly puffy ball of fur and toss it to the floor. That cat sure sheds a lot!

Dad pulls a box of tissues from a hidden storage compartment between our seats. He closes the lid before I can see what else is in there. This car has so many secrets! I hope I get to see more of them soon.

Mr. Fitch scowls and grabs the tissues. The sneezing lasts the entire way to Delta Nine.

This planet is very far away from the two suns that were so bright on Delta Three. The dim reddish light makes the planet look kind of gloomy. The leaves on the thin trees are a gray silver, and the roads have deep cracks in them. Dad quickly drives us to a downtown area and pulls up to the curb in front of a row of gray, lopsided buildings. The people walking on the street wear gray clothes and gray hats, and have gray-colored skin. They don't look unhappy, though. I guess they don't know that their planet is kind of, well, *gray*. I won't need my sunglasses here.

"You'll want to leave your gravity balls in the car," Dad tells me. "Otherwise you'd step out and sink deep into the ground."

At least this time he warned me.

With one last sneeze, Mr. Fitch grabs his briefcase and pushes open his door. "I will be back in ten minutes," he barks at us. "You will wait here."

Mr. Fitch sure is bossy! He hurries out of the car and ducks into an alley between two buildings.

Dad picks up the bags from Barney's Bagels and Schmear. "Time to eat!" We sit on the curb and dig into our sandwiches. We get some curious looks, and an occasional tip of a hat in our direction, but the people on the street mostly ignore us as they pass.

A glob of tuna falls out of my sandwich and onto the street. A second later a large cat appears out of nowhere and pounces on it. He scarfs it down in one bite. This cat is also white, like the one in the tree on the first planet. "You really do attract cats wherever you go!" Dad says, laughing.

Before I can pet this one, he must smell something he likes even better than the tuna, because he takes off in the same direction as Mr. Fitch. I swear I see a blur of green around his tail as he turns the corner. Must be a space cat thing.

Dad takes a swig from his coffee cup. "I have to check in with Home Base, Archie. Feel free to take a look around. Just make sure I can still see you, okay?"

"Got it," I say, gobbling down my pickle. Space travel makes a guy hungry. A shiny, round object lying on the street near the alley where Mr. Fitch went catches my eye. A large coin maybe? No one else has passed by that way. I wonder if he dropped it.

I turn around to ask Dad what we should do, but he's already in the taxi talking on the com line. He did say I could explore a little. With one last glance at the car, I step away from the curb and head toward the alley.

The silver object turns out to be bigger than I thought, and heavier. I turn it over in my hand. It looks like a giant locket with the letters *ISF* etched onto one smooth side. A groove runs around the edge, but I can't pry it open. Whatever it is, I bet Mr. Fitch would want it back.

I peer into the alley but can't see very far. It's dark and even gloomier than out on the streets. A loud shuffling and crashing comes from the other end of the alley. Maybe that cat knocked over a garbage can?

"Unhand me, you fool!" a man shouts. "You have no idea who you're dealing with!"

I know that bossy voice! Mr. Fitch is in trouble!

Chapter Six:
A Ratty Ball of Fur

"Let me go, I say!" Mr. Fitch shouts. "Help me, someone, help!"

It sounds like he's being robbed! Maybe someone wants his briefcase! I have to help him. Especially after I made him sneeze by petting that cat near his house. Just as I think it, Mr. Fitch starts sneezing again.

I don't want to go down there, but I have to do something. Before I change my mind, I hurl the silver disk thingy as hard as I can. All my Little League training has given me a pretty good arm, and it goes deep into the darkness. I hold my breath, wondering if I just made a huge mistake. Then I hear the object clatter to the ground and break open. The alley is immediately filled with light.

"So that's where that went," an unfamiliar voice says. I look around the alley, but the only person there besides me is Mr. Fitch. He's standing next to a pile of old boxes, blinking in the sudden light and clutching his briefcase.

"You!" he shouts, spotting me. "Space taxi kid!" He pauses to sneeze. "Get this thing off of me!"

I back up a step. "Um...what thing?"

He spins around and flails at something on his back.

My eyes open wide when I see what's actually *on* him. It's the CAT! The white cat is hanging on to the back of Mr. Fitch's suit with his claws! His tail is swishing back and forth, and I can clearly see the green circle around it. The cat sticks his head over Mr. Fitch's shoulder to look at me.

"Young sir," he says in a calm, well-mannered voice. "Thank you for returning my Light Orb. I am an officer of the ISF— that's the Intergalactic Security Force— and this man is my prisoner."

Just when I didn't think my day could get any weirder, along comes a talking cat!

I wonder if cats on Earth can talk, too, but they just hide it.

The cat continues. "If Mr. Fitch comes peacefully, he will save himself a lot of trouble."

"Not going to happen, cat!" Mr. Fitch says. Then he reaches one arm over his head and grabs the cat by the scruff of his neck.

"Look, kid," Mr. Fitch says in a calmer voice. "Who you gonna believe—me, an upstanding citizen of Delta Three, or this ratty ball of fur who must have scored a free ride in your dad's taxi to get here?"

He dangles the cat in front of him.

I step closer to get a better look. It really IS the same cat! So it wasn't my petting him that made Mr. Fitch sneeze the whole ride. It was because the cat was actually hiding IN the car with us!

"Unhand me, you brute!" the cat hollers, waving his paws in the air, claws extended. "You are under arrest for trying to sell secret documents to B.U.R.P., one of the universe's biggest criminal organizations."

"I am merely here on business," Mr. Fitch says. "Then this creature jumped on me. Now be a good boy and go tell your father I am ready to leave. And this little stowaway will be staying behind this time!"

The cat hisses.

I look from one to the other. How am I supposed to know who to believe? Mr. Fitch may be bossy, but that doesn't mean he's a criminal. And he's a grown-up, while the cat, well, he's a *cat*!

Mr. Fitch sneezes. He tightens his grip on the cat, who whimpers.

"What's it gonna be, kid?" Mr. Fitch asks in a low voice.

The cat whimpers again.

Mr. Fitch snarls.

I may not know what's really going on, but I know you shouldn't hold a cat like that. "Quick!" I tell the cat. "He's allergic to you! Ruffle your fur or something."

The cat flails his arms and legs and shimmies his body until dander and fur fly in all directions. Mr. Fitch tries to hold his breath. His face gets redder and redder until he finally has to take a breath. Then he has a massive, snot-filled sneezing fit and loosens his grip, and the cat squirms away.

"This animal doesn't know what he's talking about," Mr. Fitch says, backing away from the cat and holding up his briefcase like a shield. Peering over the top and breathing hard, he says, "There's nothing in here but boring business stuff."

Before my eyes, the cat's tail hinges open right at the green line. A laser light shoots out and zaps a hole in the briefcase! Okay, cats on Earth DEFINITELY can't do that.

Mr. Fitch yelps and drops his briefcase. It crashes to the ground and springs open. Documents marked TOP SECRET: PROPERTY OF THE ISF spill out all over the ground.

"He planted those there!" Mr. Fitch yells, stomping on them. "That cat is setting me up!"

The cat stands up on his hind legs,

unzips a pocket hidden behind a patch of gray fur, and pulls out an official badge. He holds it up so I can see his picture with the words INTERGALACTIC SECURITY FORCE OFFICER printed below it.

Mr. Fitch tries to kick at the badge. The cat twists out of the way before the heavy foot can connect with his paw. Mr. Fitch winds up losing his balance and crashes to the alley floor.

The cat points a paw straight at Mr. Fitch, and a silver rope shoots out from between two claws.

"Oomph!" Mr. Fitch says as the rope tightens around his wrists and ankles. Then he has another sneezing fit.

The cat runs over to me, stands on two legs, and shakes my hand.

At that moment my father rounds the corner of the alley. His eyes widen as he takes in the scene. Then he smiles and shakes his head. "You know, Archie, if you wanted to get a cat this badly, you could have just asked."

We all laugh. Well, not Mr. Fitch.

CHAPTER SEVEN:
A New Job

"Intergalactic Security Force officer Pilarbing Fangorious Catapolitus at your service," the cat says, bowing to my father. "Sorry about stowing away in your trunk." To me he says, "I am grateful for your aid, young Earth boy. You are very brave. I will see to it that you are well rewarded."

I blush and finish gathering up the papers while the cat—whose name is way too long for me to remember—tells my dad the whole story. Dad agrees to bring the space cat and his captive to ISF headquarters.

The cat leads a red-faced and sneezing Mr. Fitch into the backseat and buckles him in. Then he nudges him with the tip of his pink nose and Mr. Fitch immediately falls into a deep sleep. That's a handy trick! Maybe I could use that on Penny when she wants to play one more game of pretend-Archie-is-a-horsie.

"How are you holding up?" Dad asks me as we strap ourselves in.

"I'm fine. You know, just a regular day. I copilot a space taxi, almost float off a planet, talk to a cat, help catch a criminal. And all before breakfast!"

He laughs. "It's not over yet."

As I smooth out my map, I ask, "Hey, can the cats on Earth talk, too?"

He shakes his head. "Nope. Only the ones from Friskopolus, otherwise known as the Cat Planet. That's where we're headed now."

Dad tells me the coordinates, and I ask the map to show me Friskopolus. Lines shoot out from the image of the little taxi and I quickly plan out the route. I don't want to brag, but I'm getting good at this. I whisper "thank you" to the map, and it almost seems to quiver a bit in response. Then again, I haven't slept in a really long time.

"So, Cat," Dad says once we're on our way, "how did you know Fitch was headed here?"

The cat pauses from cleaning behind his ear with his paw to answer. "I've been tracking him for months. Following him in my own police car would have been much too suspicious. I'd given up hope until you two came along and I saw my chance. I won't forget you and what you've done to help bring peace to the universe."

"We won't forget you, either," I say. "Um, what was your name again?"

"Pilarbing Fangorious Catapolitus," the cat replies.

I glance at Dad. He shrugs.

I turn back to the cat. "That's a big name for a little cat. Or even a big cat, like you. Do you have a nickname?"

The cat shakes his head.

"Okay. How about I call you...Mr. Bubbles!"

The cat frowns, which is something space cats must be able to do.

"Fluffy?"

He narrows his eyes at me.

"Hmm. You probably won't like Snowball, then."

The cat growls.

Dad and I laugh. "Just kidding," I say. "I'll try to come up with a really good name for a space police cat."

I sit back and enjoy watching all the stars glitter around us like billions and billions of fireflies. It might be years before I get to see this view again. Maybe when I grow up, I could get a job with Dad. That would be so awesome.

Mr. Fitch's snoring from the backseat is actually kind of soothing.

I hear a rustling behind me and turn to look. The cat is digging around in his fur pockets. He pulls out a pair of dark sunglasses and slips them on.

"That's it!" I shout. "I'll call you Pockets!"

The cat shrugs. "That is acceptable."

"What else have you got in there?" I ask, peering over the seat.

"Ah, the question should be what *don't* I have in there." He lifts his shades with one paw and winks at me.

I smile and turn back around. I can see from the map that we're about to reach the planet's atmosphere. A few minutes later our wheels touch down on a busy landing field behind Intergalactic Security Force headquarters. Spaceships and space police cars of all different shapes and sizes are landing and taking off.

We are met by two giant cats wearing official ISF badges around their necks. They place a groggy Mr. Fitch onto the back of a little buggy and drive away with him.

Dad and I follow Pockets into the main building. I have to step over large bowls of water and dishes of cat food scattered across the floor. Little robotic mice dart between our legs. The walls are made of yarn. Cats even bigger and fluffier than Pockets are happily eating, licking their paws, chasing fake mice and each other, and scratching the walls. Some are doing this while holding clipboards or talking on the phone.

"Is everyone in the ISF a cat?" I whisper to Pockets.

He shakes his head. "There are headquarters on one planet in each galaxy. We all work together to bring down B.U.R.P. and help keep the universe safe."

"What does B.U.R.P. even stand for?" I ask.

"No one knows," he admits. "It's a big mystery."

We wind up in a large office where a cat who looks like an older, more grizzled version of Pockets is pacing back and forth, a worried look on his face.

"Hello, Father," Pockets says. "I'm back."

The older cat stops pacing and races over to us. He looks Pockets up and down, then jumps on him and flips him over! Dad and I back away. They meow and roll over each other, swatting each other playfully on the nose.

"I was very worried," his father says, stopping to nuzzle Pockets under the chin with his head.

Pockets bats his father away. "I'm fine, Chief. This was my twentieth mission! Didn't you receive my report? I sent it from the space taxi."

"Yes, I got it. You've always been independent, but it's a parent's job to worry about their child."

"Will you still worry about me like that?" I ask Dad. "When I'm all grown up?"

Before my dad can answer, Pockets says, "Well . . . I'm not exactly all grown up."

"You're not?" I ask.

He shakes his head. "I'm only eight years old."

"You're only eight?" Dad and I shout at the same time.

"That's *my* age!" I add. "You sound a lot more grown up than me. And you can do a LOT more things."

"I was always very advanced for my age," Pockets admits. "My father here is the head of the agency, the chief detective on the force. Everyone knew I'd join one day, so I've been training since I was a small kitten. But enough about me." Turning to his father, he says, "You've read my report, Chief. What do you think about my request?"

The chief looks at me and Dad. "Well, I suppose that's up to the humans to decide."

"What are we deciding?" Dad asks.

The chief clears a hair ball from his throat. "It seems my son here thinks you and *your* son would be very helpful in our mission to take down B.U.R.P. before they're able to take over the universe. You'd be honorary Intergalactic Security Force deputies."

My eyes widen. First I discover I'm a space taxi copilot, then I get to help fight intergalactic crime? This has *got* to be the BEST Take Your Kid to Work Day in the history of the universe. I clutch my dad's arm. "That sounds awesome, doesn't it, Dad? Wait till I tell the kids at school!"

Dad hesitates. "Archie, I know it sounds exciting, but we don't know anything about catching criminals."

"We understand that," the chief says. "But Pilarbing Fangorious thinks—"

"We call him Pockets," I interrupt. "Easier to say."

The chief tilts his head at me. "All right, then. *Pockets* thinks, and I agree, that he would blend in easier if he pretended to be merely a child's pet. Adults say things in front of kids that they would not normally say, and that could come in very handy when spying on a suspect. Also, your space taxi is a perfect mode of transportation. It's fast, it can travel to every corner of the universe, and it doesn't need special permission to land. It would be the perfect cover for our secret missions."

"I'd really like to help you," Dad says.

"But if Archie came on my route with me every night, he'd be too tired to go to school. His education is too important."

Before I can think of an argument to counter that, Pockets steps forward. "I can speak three thousand languages," he says. "And what I know about history and math and science and literature could fill a hundred school libraries. I could teach him when we get home each morning—after he sleeps, of course."

"When *we* get home each morning?" my dad repeats.

"My son would have to come live with you," the chief explains. "He's still a kid, after all. Someone would have to watch over him."

I squeal, which is a little dorky, but I

can't help it. My own crime-fighting cat? How awesome would that be? "Can we do it, Dad? You said you don't have a copilot anymore, and don't you need one? Think of all the things I could learn on the job that I'd never be able to learn in school."

Dad sighs. "I did hope you'd be my copilot one day, Archie, but I thought that day would be far from now. I'll agree to a week and we'll see what happens." He shakes his head. "I don't know what your mom's gonna say about this."

"Yay!" I jump up and down. A week is better than nothing. I'm getting a cat PLUS a friend my own age to hang out with, all rolled into one! And I'll be helping to save the universe every night! Pockets holds his paw up to me.

"High five!" we both say at the same time.

"You wouldn't actually be able to tell your schoolmates about this," Pockets says, suddenly serious again. "Our mission has to remain top secret."

After a flash of disappointment I say, "I understand. I promise."

We high-five again and I can't control my grin.

I turn to my dad. "Thanks for agreeing to this! I bet after a few days Mom will get used to having an alien living with us."

"Oh, it wouldn't be the first time," he says.

I pause. "What do you mean?"

"Bubba from Belora Prime lived under

our kitchen sink for a few weeks while his house was being painted."

My eyes widen, then narrow. "Did he have four arms and three eyes?"

Dad nods.

"I *knew* it!"

Chapter Eight:
Home, Sweet Home

Dad gasses up the taxi while Pockets goes back to his house to get his suitcase. A thick layer of dirt and grime and things that look like barnacles cover the car. Now I understand why Dad washes his taxi every day.

When Pockets shows up at the landing field, he doesn't have anything with him. I hope he hasn't changed his mind.

"Aren't you still coming home with us?" I ask.

He nods.

"Then where's all your stuff?"

He pats his chest and belly. "Right here."

I laugh. "Those are some big pockets!"

Pockets grins, then goes over to his father and nuzzles him under the neck. His father nuzzles him back.

"We'll take good care of him," my dad promises. "And I'll make sure he checks in with you daily."

"He's very good at that," the chief says, getting a little teary. He gives his son one final nuzzle, then turns his attention to Dad. "Now, Morningstar, when you're on a mission, Pilarbing Fang—I mean, *Pockets* is in command. During off-hours, *you* are in control. I'll be meeting with my staff tomorrow to figure out how to make the best use of you."

Watching Dad awkwardly shake the chief's paw is kind of funny. I don't think it would be polite to laugh, though, so I turn it into a cough.

When we get into the taxi, the voice coming out of the invisible speakers is screeching like someone who just stepped with bare feet on hot sand. "This is Home Base!" the voice squeaks angrily. "Morningstar, do you hear me? Repeat, do you hear me?"

"She doesn't sound happy, Dad."

"I've been avoiding calling in," Dad admits. "How could I tell them that my fare turned out to be a criminal and was arrested and I had to make an unscheduled stop with him out cold in my backseat?"

"What did you just say?" the voice screeches in an even higher pitch than usual.

"Oops," Dad says. "Guess I left the com line open." He clears his throat. "Hello, Home Base. I'll explain everything when I get back. Morningstar out." He leans over and turns off the knob just as she screeches, "Oh, no you don't, mister!"

Dad winks and asks, "Are you boys strapped in?"

"Yup," I say.

"Indeed I am," Pockets replies.

As we take off, I turn to Dad and ask, "Why does that Home Base lady have such a squeaky voice? She kinda sounds like a mouse."

Dad laughs. "Not *kinda* like a mouse. She IS a mouse!"

At that, Pockets's ears perk up. "A mouse?" he says. "I've never seen a real one!"

"Don't get any ideas back there," Dad warns, but he's smiling. "That mouse is my boss. That means you two will be working together very closely, Pockets. And *that* means no eating each other."

Pockets mutters something that sounds like "I'd like to see *her* try to eat *me*." Then he reaches into one of his pockets, pulls out a full-size pillow (!), and curls up for a nap.

While he sleeps, Dad and I finally eat the breakfasts Mom packed for us. I gobble down three delicious pancakes. Penny only eats things that start with the letter *P*, so we have a lot of pancakes. I'll eat pretty much anything except broccoli, because why would I want to eat something that looks like a tree? We clink thermoses before taking sips. After traveling millions of light-years from home, my hot chocolate is still warm!

I spend the rest of the trip exploring my map. If I turn it in different directions, it shows me all sorts of amazing things. I can't wait to see what pops up on my next trip. I direct us into the right worm-hole to get us back. This time I try to keep my eyes open, even on the stomach-churning parts. The bright colors streak by on all sides. One of them—the red streak—moves more slowly than the rest.

A second later it's right next to the taxi. I push my face against the window to get a better look. Then I jump back in surprise.

A tiny red alien in a tiny bubble-shaped spaceship just WAVED at me! I blink and he's gone. I shake my head. "Um, Dad? Did you happen to see a little red alien outside my window?"

He shakes his head. "Nope. But all these lights can play tricks on your eyes."

"I guess you're right," I say, peering into the emptiness around us.

"You did a great job today, Archie," Dad says. "I'm very proud of you." He reaches over and ruffles my hair.

Normally that would embarrass me, but now it just makes me feel good. "Thank you for trusting me to be your copilot, Dad."

He grins. "When I promised you tonight would be an adventure, I had no idea how right I would be."

I grin back. "Yeah, Dad, you left out a lot of stuff about tonight."

He laughs, then gets serious. "I wanted to tell you everything, Archie. But I had to wait until you were old enough to understand. I think you and I make a great team."

I glance into the backseat at the sleeping cat. We're a team of three now.

Once I get us back through Earth's atmosphere, I roll up my map. I wish I had some way to carry it with me. It's not the kind of thing I can just stick in my pocket, like a certain cat I know. I need a way to keep it safe.

As we get closer to Earth, I see a single bright star hanging alone in the sky, glittering like a diamond. Suddenly I know *exactly* what I need. I reach behind me and feel around on the floor until I find my tube from Grandpa. I pop open the top and slide the map inside. A perfect fit!

"I was waiting for you to figure that out," Dad says, smiling. Then he points east at a ball of light. "Do you know what that is?"

"It's Venus, right? The Morning Star?"

"Indeed it is." Dad aims the taxi so I have the perfect view out the front window. The air around Venus glows with the light of the rising sun. Maybe my last

name isn't so bad. After all, it's the name of a long line of space taxi drivers. And also copilots. And now honorary Intergalactic Security Force deputies saving the universe from the evil B.U.R.P., which, when you think about it, is a much worse name than mine.

Behind me, Pockets yawns and stretches. "Anyone got some tuna?"

Three Science Facts to Impress Your Friends and Teachers

1. Gravity is the invisible force that attracts two objects. The heavier the object, the more gravity it has. Gravity is what keeps the planets in orbit around the sun and keeps all the stuff on Earth from floating into space. The planet called Delta Three that Archie visits in this book is smaller than Earth and weighs less, so it has less gravity. The people who live there are taller, the trees are taller, and it's easier for birds to fly and people to walk.

2. A WORMHOLE is like a tunnel from one part of outer space to another. Picture an apple—it would take a worm less time to go through a hole in the apple than to go around the skin of the apple. Some scientists believe this kind of a shortcut through space might one day be possible.

3. Even though we don't think of it this way, our sun is actually a star. It's just a lot closer to us than any other star. A planet that orbits a star *other* than our own sun is called an EXOPLANET. In order for life as we know it to exist, a planet must not be too close to or too far away from its source of heat (its sun) so that its temperature stays within a certain zone. It needs to have water, oxygen, an atmosphere around it, and the right kinds of chemicals in the ground and air. But that's only life as we know it here on Earth. Other planets could have people or creatures living there that have adapted to their environment as we have adapted to ours. With the help of huge telescopes, astronomers are discovering new exoplanets every day. Someday soon we will surely discover that we are not alone in the vast universe.

SPACE TAXI

WATER PLANET RESCUE

By Wendy Mass and Michael Brawer

Illustrated by Elise Gravel

LITTLE, BROWN AND COMPANY
New York   Boston

Dedicated to our giant cat, Bubba,
the inspiration for Pockets.
He's not as smart as Pockets, though.
And the only thing he can hide in his fur
is more fur.

CONTENTS

CHAPTER ONE:
Cats Don't Swim

I know everyone thinks their family is strange, but seriously, mine has them all beat. First of all, my dad drives a taxi in OUTER SPACE! Second of all, *I'm* somehow able to read the space map that helps him get from planet to planet. And third, since my little sister, Penny, only eats things that start with the letter *P*, I had to eat a persimmon for dessert last night. A persimmon is kind of like a cross between a mango and a tomato, only not as good as either a mango or a tomato. I asked Mom why we couldn't have popcorn (also starts with a *P*) instead, but she said if she has to pop one more batch of popcorn, she's going to run screaming through the neighborhood in her nightgown.

See? I told you. Weird family!

But I haven't even gotten to the weirdest part yet. A few days ago we got a talking cat from another planet. Pockets helps protect the universe as an Intergalactic Security Force officer. We call him Pockets because he can fit almost anything into pockets hidden behind patches of fur on his belly. And also his real name is way too long to remember.

Pockets made Dad and me deputies of the Intergalactic Security Force (called the ISF for short) because we helped him catch a criminal and sort of save the universe at the same time.

The ISF needs Dad to be available whenever Pockets has a mission for us, so his regular space taxi job is on hold awhile. I had expected Dad to grumble about this because he loves driving his taxi, but nope. He's totally into being home all the time. Two days ago he fixed that crack in the wall in our kitchen (but made a new one on the floor by dropping a brick). Then he painted the family room green (and dripped paint all over Mom's favorite chair), and tried to put up a shelf but only made two really big holes in the wall, which Mom had to cover with an old, broken clock.

Yesterday he took us to the zoo, where Penny got scared by the butterfly exhibit and cried until we got kicked out for upsetting the other kids. Today we're going swimming. Hopefully nothing will go wrong at the pool, but the odds are against it.

Truthfully? I'm itching to get back to outer space, and I *know* Mom is ready for Dad to get back to work.

"Got your suit on, Archie?" Dad calls out from the hall. "The pool opens in half an hour."

"Coming!" I grab my ISF badge and

my space map and tuck them into my pool bag. ISF deputy Archie Morningstar is ALWAYS ready for duty. Mom said she'll only let me do this job if I promise to look before I leap and always listen to Dad and Pockets. She says I don't "think things through," because of one trip (okay, *four* trips) to the principal's office last year due to a series of science projects that didn't work out as expected. The janitor was able to get the scorch marks off the ceiling after only a few weeks of scrubbing, so really, I don't see what all the fuss was about.

When I get to the living room I spot Pockets asleep in his favorite sunny spot on the window ledge. That cat sure sleeps a lot. And he sheds a TON. Our apartment is covered in clumps of white fur. It sticks to the carpet and hangs from the walls (still wet from the paint) and lampshades and furniture. I don't know how one cat can shed so much. Mom's vacuum cleaner is lying on the floor, broken. Clearly, it was no match for all this fur.

You wouldn't know it from all the shedding, but Pockets likes things to be neat and orderly. He cleans up my room every time I leave it. I haven't told Mom yet that it's not my doing. She'll figure it out soon enough.

"This is NOT what I signed up for," a voice growls from behind me. I turn around to see Pockets frowning up at me, his paws on his hips. He's wearing a pair of my old yellow swim trunks and Penny's purple goggles. I turn back to look at the

TODAY IN FELINE FASHION

window ledge, where I can swear I'm look-ing at Pockets asleep, then back again to the cat behind me. I rub my eyes to make sure I'm fully awake.

"If you're here," I ask him as my dad walks into the room, "then who's that sleeping by the window? Do you have a

117

twin? Can you clone yourself?" Do I now have TWO talking pet cats?

Dad strides across the room and pokes at the sleeping cat on the ledge. His finger goes right through! It's not a cloned space cat after all. It's a Pockets-shaped ball of fur! I admit I'm a little disappointed.

Dad lifts up the huge pile of fur. "This," he announces, "is the sign of a cat who needs a good grooming."

"How do we know that's mine?" Pockets asks, crossing his paws in front of him.

Dad and I raise our eyebrows at him.

"All right, all right," Pockets says, walking toward Dad. "I can't help it. Something in the air on your planet makes my fur grow very quickly." He waves the dangling fluff ball away, and white fur flies in all directions. I sneeze as a few pieces fly up my nose. I consider reminding him that he shed a lot before he even got to Earth, but he looks like he's in kind of a dark mood.

"Can we focus on the larger problem here?" Pockets demands. He points to his swim shorts with one front paw and to his goggles with the other.

Dad turns to me. "I don't see a problem with the way Pockets looks," he says. "Do you, Archie?"

I try hard not to giggle. "He looks like a cat who's ready to go swimming."

Dad nods. "My thoughts exactly, son."

Pockets tries to pull off his goggles, but they just snap back in his face. "I am a highly respected Intergalactic Security Force officer," he says, puffing out his chest.

"I have won medals for bravery on more missions than I can count. But one thing I do NOT do is swim."

"Why not?" I ask.

"Cats don't swim," he replies.

"But why not?" I ask.

"They just don't," he snaps.

Dad puts his arm around Pockets. "We're only fooling with you. Of course you don't have to come. In fact, the pool doesn't allow pets. You were a very good sport to let Penny dress you up this way."

Pockets seems calmed by Dad's words. He shrugs. "No harm, I suppose. The worst part was having to keep my mouth shut."

"I know it's hard pretending to be a regular cat around Penny," Dad says, "but we've been over this. She's too young to keep your secret identity as a crime-fighting cat from outer space. What if she told her friends at preschool? They'd tell their parents, and your cover would be blown."

Personally, I don't think we have to worry about this, because Penny only says, like, three words. And never in a row.

"I understand," Pockets says. "I am a trained professional. I can pretend to be a house pet, easy. See?" He begins to purr and rubs up against Dad's leg like a regular cat. With a swish of his tail, he walks away, leaving a thick coating of white fur behind.

Dad looks down at his fur-covered legs. "Guess we're making a stop on the way to the pool. That cat's getting a haircut!"

CHAPTER TWO:
What's Better Than a Bath?

Pockets's goggles won't come off. They are tangled in his fur. We can't even use scissors without worrying about poking him. I'm sure he has some kind of alien gadget hidden in one of his pockets that would fix it, but since Penny's with us, he just has to wait for the groomer to deal with it.

He basically pouts and growls the whole way there in Dad's taxi until Penny leans out of her car seat and starts to pet him. Then he starts to purr. She kisses him on the head and he rubs against her hand. Mom says Penny could charm the rattles off a snake.

Dad parks around the corner from the groomer's. I unstrap Pockets and half drag, half carry him out of the car. Penny waves good-bye. "Have a nice bath!" Mom calls out her window. As soon as we're out of sight of the car, Pockets springs from my arms. He grabs something the size of a pen from one of his pockets.

"Oomph!" Dad says, banging his face on what looks like thin air. He backs up, then reaches out with his hand to feel in front of him. I reach out, too. My hand hits what feels like a solid wall!

"What's going on here?" Dad asks, knocking on the invisible surface.

I shake my head at Pockets as he casually slips his pen-like device back into a pocket. "Did you put up an invisible force field?"

Pockets doesn't bother to deny it. "I certainly did! You never said anything about a bath. You know how I feel about water."

Dad rubs his nose. "You're making too big a deal about this. It'll be over before you know it."

"I do not need a bath!" Pockets insists. "I can clean myself just fine." He proceeds to lick his arm repeatedly. Then he stops, coughs, and hacks up a slimy hairball. It plops onto the sidewalk at our feet.

We stare at it. Pockets's cheeks turn red.

I rest my hand on his shoulder. "I'm

pretty sure you don't want to do *that* in front of the next criminal you try to arrest."

Pockets sighs. "Fine. I shall submit to the bath." He begins emptying his pockets. One by one, he thrusts gadgets and gizmos of all sizes and shapes into our arms. Some things I recognize, like rope and a notebook and a compass. But most of it I don't. I glance around to make sure no one on the street can see us.

"Aren't your pockets waterproof?" Dad asks as our arms fill up.

"I don't want to take any chances with your Earth water," Pockets explains. "Who knows what's in it. No offense, of course." Finally, he pulls out two big black bags, and we stuff everything inside.

"The groomer will be very careful while giving you the bath," Dad promises, hefting the bags over his shoulders. "They do this all day."

"*What*?" Pockets asks, his eyes almost popping out of his face. "Someone GIVES ME THE BATH?"

"Of course," Dad says. "That's part of the groomer's job."

Pockets throws up his paws. "That's it! I'm asking my father for a raise the next time I see him!"

He lets me pick him up without further complaint. This time there's no force field keeping us from entering the groomer's, but Dad walks with his hands out in front of us just to make sure.

"That's one fluffy cat you have," the groomer says as I plop Pockets on the counter. "Pockets Morningstar, right?"

"That's right," Dad replies. "He's very excited to be here."

Pockets flexes one paw, revealing five dagger-sharp claws.

The woman's eyes widen. "We'll be taking care of those, don't you worry. We have special scissors for cutting nails."

Pockets looks at me, his eyes pleading. He needs those claws to be the best police cat he can be.

"Um, maybe you shouldn't clip his claws," I tell the groomer. "He needs those to, you know, climb stuff."

The woman frowns. "He doesn't go outside in the city, does he? That's very dangerous for a cat."

I shake my head. "No, but he likes to, um, climb the curtains in our living room."

This is actually true.

She raises her eyebrows. "And you want him to continue doing that?"

Dad steps in now. "Oh, yes. We think it's very good exercise. As you can see, he could stand to lose a few pounds."

Pockets shoots Dad a look, and I allow myself a giggle.

"Suit yourself," she says, and slides some forms across the counter for Dad to sign. "He'll be ready in an hour. But you can pick him up anytime before five." Then she scoops up Pockets and they disappear behind a curtain. A trail of white fur is all that's left of him.

I don't talk much on the way to the community center, where the indoor pool is located. I can't help feeling kind of bad leaving him there while the rest of us are going to have fun swimming.

Only a few other families are at the pool. Dad tosses colorful plastic hoops into the deep end and I swim down and get them. I wish I could dive in, but I've never been able to do it without landing on my belly. Mom

and Penny are splashing around in the shallow end. Penny loves putting her hand up to the water jets and laughs as the force of the water pushes her hand away. That girl may not talk, but she sure can laugh.

I join them for a few minutes, and Penny and I play a game to see who can keep their hand in front of the jet the longest. She always wins.

I swim back to the deep end. I can't stop thinking about Pockets and how sad he looked. "Think he's okay at the groomer's?" I ask Dad as I hand a red hoop up to him.

"I'm sure he's fine," Dad says. "You heard him. He's had adventures all across the universe. He can handle getting a haircut."

I'm about to swim under for the next ring when a blur running alongside the pool catches my eye.

The blur skids to a stop. Water and bubbles fly everywhere.

It's Pockets! He's still wearing Penny's purple goggles. Soap bubbles cling to his fur in wet clumps. Dad grabs for the watch that he placed on the side of the pool, before Pockets can knock it into the water.

"I can't believe it," Dad says. "You broke out of the groomer's?"

"How did you find us?" I ask, kind of impressed. I'm pretty sure no one told him the address of the pool.

Pockets does this head-to-tail shimmying thing. Soapy water flies out in all directions. His fur doesn't look any shorter. "No time to explain, my good deputies. We've got a mission!"

Chapter Three:
Akbar's Floating Rest Stop

One of the perks of being a taxi driver (even a space taxi driver) is that you can always get a ride when you need one. It only takes a few minutes before one of Dad's friends arrives to take Mom and Penny home.

Dad hooks up Penny's car seat in the

back while Mom fusses over me. I know she's not too happy with my new job, but being a copilot is a Morningstar family tradition. You can't argue with tradition.

"Promise you'll be careful up there," she says, hugging me tight. "Do what Dad and Pockets tell you."

I hug her back until Dad honks for me.

I'm so excited that my legs won't stop bouncing in my seat. Or maybe I'm just cold because I'm in a wet bathing suit. Nah, I'm excited! Our first official mission!

"All right, Pockets," Dad says once we're headed toward the airfield. "What's this all about? Start from when we dropped you at the groomer's."

I twist around in my seat and wait for Pockets to answer. He's refilling his pockets with all his gadgets. "It is pretty simple, really," he says. "In the middle of my so-called *bath*, the tiny interlink hidden inside my ear started beeping. It was my father calling from ISF headquarters. He said that the planet Nautilus in the Triangulum Galaxy is experiencing a very strange weather situation. We are the nearest officers, so we're being sent to check it out and file a report."

"You're not making this up just to get out of the bath, are you?" Dad asks. He narrows his eyes at Pockets.

"Of course not," Pockets says. "I'm as disappointed as you are about the bath being cut short." His lips quiver and I know he's trying to hide a smile.

"I'm sure," Dad says.

"How did you find us?" I ask. "I bet it was some supercool locator device that lets you track people down anywhere on the planet with a press of a button, right?"

"Nope," Pockets says, tapping his nose. "Cats have an excellent sense of smell, you know. You should probably bathe more often. No offense."

It's hard not to be offended when someone basically says you stink so bad they could track your scent across town. "Well, *you* don't like baths, either," I remind him.

"I told you," he says. "Cats are self-cleaning."

I glance at his matted, tangled fur. "Is that a leaf stuck to your tail?"

He turns around in circles in his seat, trying to catch his tail, but he can't. I start to laugh, then reach over to pull the leaf off for him.

"Thanks," he grumbles.

"Boys," Dad says. "You can argue about who needs a bath more when we get home. Right now we have to prepare for the mission."

The com line crackles with a call from Home Base. "Morningstar!" the female mouse squeaks. She comes from a planet where mice can talk, and it's her job to keep track of all the space taxis. Dad told me her name is Minerva. He warned me not to call her Minnie for short, though. One of the newer space taxi drivers made the mistake of calling her *Minnie the Mouse*— or *Minnie Mouse* for short. She didn't like being compared to a cartoon character, so she sent the poor guy to pick up a fare on an ice planet where the temperature was two hundred degrees below zero. It took him a week to thaw out.

I can't wait to meet her.

"We have received your information from the ISF," she continues. At the sound of Minerva's squeaky voice, Pockets's ears stand at alert and his nose twitches. "We have cleared the airfield and made arrangements for you to stop at Akbar's Floating Rest Stop on the way to the planet Nautilus. You will get some special mods for your visit there."

"Roger that," Dad says.

The voice continues. "We miss you at Home Base. Some of your usual fares aren't happy about your... ahem, *vacation*."

"Things will be back to business as usual soon, I'm sure," Dad says.

"Are you certain you can trust this... this *cat*?" she asks, unable to hide her dislike. Turns out cats and mice are sworn enemies everywhere in the universe, not just on Earth.

"I can hear you, you know," Pockets calls from the backseat. He has pulled out a towel and is trying to dry his wet, matted fur.

"I trust him," Dad assures her.

"Fine," she snaps. "You are cleared for takeoff. As usual, be careful up there."

"Always am," Dad says. "Morningstar over and out."

The second set of straps pins us to our seats and the taxi speeds up.

"What are mods?" I have to shout over the noise of the engine.

"Modifications," my dad shouts back. "Changes we need to make to the taxi."

I grip the seat as the front tires lift off the ground and we begin to zoom toward the blue sky. I forgot how fast we go at takeoff. I swallow hard and wait to catch my breath before shouting over the roar of the rocket boosters. "Why do you need to change anything? What's wrong with the taxi?"

"Nothing," Dad yells, pulling down on the throttle as we pass through the clouds. "Nautilus is a water planet. Our space taxi will need to become a space submarine."

Underwater Deputy Archie Morningstar has a nice ring to it! "Do you always have to do this when you go to Nautilus?" I ask.

He shakes his head. "I've been to Akbar's for repairs many times, but I've never been to Nautilus."

This surprises me. Hasn't my dad been everywhere? "But I thought your job took you all over the universe."

"The universe is a really big place, Archie," he says as the taxi picks up speed.

"Even after all these years of traveling through it, I've only seen a tiny slice."

I turn to look behind us. The sun is now a small glowing blob as we head out of the solar system.

"This would be a good time to start guiding us to Akbar's," Dad says. "It's orbiting near the outer arm of the Milky Way."

I stowed the tube under the backseat earlier this morning. Pockets hands it to me, and I hurry to unroll the map. Then I stop. What if my being able to read the map was a one-time thing? What if all I see are dots and squiggles again and Dad has to go back to Earth to find a real space taxi copilot?

I guess I'm about to find out. I lay the map open in my lap and hold my breath.

Nothing happens. I focus on the paper, silently begging it to work. A few seconds later the map springs to life, sending stars and planets into the air above my lap.

PHEW!

"Akbar's Floating Rest Stop, please," I say out loud. The map zooms in on a small object out past a triple star system. I scan the area to see the best route. "Okay, Dad. Left past the third red star, then a quick right."

Dad follows my instructions, and we're on our way.

"Good job, Archie," he says.

"So what's the big weather emergency, anyway?" I ask Pockets.

"Nautilus is covered in water," Pockets tells us. "Half the people live under the ocean, and the other half live on islands they built on the surface. But the water level is going down fast. No one knows why. That's what we're going to find out."

"How are we going to do that?" Dad asks.

"Because *I'm* on the case."

Pockets is a very confident cat.

A few minutes later we approach what looks like a gigantic shopping mall floating in space. A huge flashing billboard sticking out of the top announces: AKBAR'S FLOATING REST STOP, FOR ALL YOUR TRAVEL NEEDS. Then underneath, in smaller (but still huge) letters, it says: IF YOU LIVED HERE, YOU'D BE HOME NOW. Then in even smaller (but still really big) letters it says: JUST KIDDING. YOU CAN'T LIVE HERE. BUT STOP BY FOR A VISIT. WE'RE ALWAYS OPEN.

My eyes open wider and wider as we soar past flashing neon signs for the bathrooms, the snack bar, the gift shop, the game room, and, most surprising of all, a Barney's Bagels and Schmear restaurant! All the way out here!

On every side of the huge floating building are long metal arms with hand-like clamps on the ends. Most of the arms have spaceships of different sizes and shapes attached to them. Dad steers the taxi toward an empty pair of metal arms. The arms reach out toward the taxi and clamp onto our front bumper. The taxi gives a small shudder, and then Dad turns off the engine. He flips on the com line. "Salazar Morningstar," he announces. Then adds, "And friends."

"Greetings, Mr. Morningstar," a friendly voice replies. "Please state the purpose of your visit to Akbar's today."

"We have an appointment at Graff's Garage," Dad says.

"Please stay seated," the voice instructs. The taxi begins to glide along the side of the building, and I crane my neck to see out the window. The metal arms are moving us to another spot. One final jolt and we stop. Then two large metal doors slide open and our car is pulled inside the building. When we stop, we're about twenty feet above the ground. A blinking sign announces: WELCOME TO GRAFF'S GARAGE. IF WE CAN'T FIX IT, IT AIN'T BROKE.

"Enjoy your visit," the pleasant voice says. "And don't forget to get a bagel from Barney's on your way out."

Pockets licks his lips and says, "This Barney's location has the best tuna fish sandwich this side of the Milky Way. Yuuuumy!" He rubs his still-damp belly. That cat sure does love his tuna.

"You've been here before, too?" I ask.

"Everyone's been to Akbar's Rest Stop," Pockets replies. "Come, let's get the taxi fixed up so we can get to the tuna!"

"And to Nautilus," I add.

"Yes, of course," Pockets says, but doesn't take his eyes off the sign for Barney's.

I peer out the windshield. We're nowhere near the ground. Before I can warn him, Pockets flings open his door and steps out.

CHAPTER FOUR:

Graff's Garage

"Pockets!" I shout, my heart racing. I throw open my door and look all around. I don't see him anywhere.

"Down here," a voice calls out.

Pockets! I whip my head around until I find him standing on a movable sidewalk that runs along the opposite side of the car. He waves as the sidewalk glides him toward a door in the middle of the wall marked GARAGE.

Phew!

Dad chuckles and I realize he's holding on to the back of my bathing suit. "At least you didn't try to climb out your own door," he says, letting go. "The sidewalk's only on the driver's side."

I scramble over and follow Dad out onto the moving walkway. I try not to think about what would have happened if I had hopped out my own door with nowhere to go but the floor far below. Penny would take my bedroom, that's for sure. She would pull down my maps of the city and replace them with pictures of unicorns and fairies and mermaids. I shudder at the thought.

The sidewalk takes us into a large

mechanic's shop loaded with equipment and vehicles. Whirring, beeping, grinding, and banging sounds bounce off the high ceiling. It would look just like any big mechanic's shop at home if it weren't for the fact that the workers all appear to be giant man-size ants with hard black shells and antennae that wave from their heads as they work.

I shrink back. I still have nightmares from dropping an ant farm when I was in kindergarten. It totally wasn't my fault, by the way. The floor was wet from spilled juice, and anyone would have slipped on it. (Although, now that I think of it, the juice may have been my fault.) The tiny ants flew *everywhere*. Mom was picking them out of my hair for days.

The tallest of the ant guys spots us and waves one long arm. He hops off a ladder and slides a wrench into a pocket hanging off his belt. "Sal Morningstar!" he says in exactly the kind of chirpy voice you would think an ant would have, only deeper. "How you doin', man?"

Dad smiles and reaches for one of the guy's four hands. A stream of oozy grease slides onto Dad's hand as they shake. It came right out of the guy's wrist! Up close I can see they aren't really giant ants, only ant-*like*. Turns out the antennae on their heads are tools attached to a hat. They have regular ears on the sides of their heads. Still, I'm sticking close to Dad.

"Good to see you, Graff," Dad says, wiping his grease-smeared hand on his pants. "Been a long time." He puts his other hand on my shoulder. "This is my son, Archie. He's my copilot now."

Graff's large round eyes shine down at me. "Congratulations, young Morningstar. That's a big responsibility."

I force myself to smile, but it comes out kind of shaky. "I know," I say. And then I blurt out, "We save the universe now, too."

Dad stares at me.

I put my hand over my mouth. Oops! Maybe Dad should worry about *me* giving our secrets away, not Penny.

"Anyway," Dad says, quickly changing the subject, "you got the message we were coming?"

"Sure did," Graff says. "We're all ready for you."

At that moment Pockets jumps out from behind me, where I didn't even realize he had been crouching. Is he going to yell at me for saying that thing about saving the universe? Or worse yet, fire us? I was really hoping to get a chance to foil some more crimes.

But he runs right past me, leaps onto Graff's shoulders, and tackles him to the ground! Graff yelps in surprise. Clumps of wet fur and sticky grease fly in all directions as they wrestle. I feel like I should probably do something, but I'm so surprised that I can't seem to move.

The two roll around on the ground meowing (Pockets) and chirping (Graff). Dad rushes over, shouting at Pockets to stop. But before he reaches them, they stand up, dust themselves off, and start laughing.

Graff clasps Pockets on the shoulder. "You looked a lot better the last time I saw you, young Pilarbing Fangorious!" Graff says, grinning. "What happened to you?"

Pockets tries to smooth himself down, but it doesn't do any good. He really is a mess. Besides his clumpy wet fur, he now has black grease all over him.

Pockets points one paw at Dad. "*He* thought I needed a bath."

"I would definitely agree with that," Graff says, laughing again.

"So," Dad says, scratching his head. "I'm guessing you two know each other?"

Graff nods. A glob of grease squirts out of the joint in his neck. I try not to stare. "I've known Pilarbing since he was a tiny kitten," he explains. "His father is an old friend. Looks like he's got some new friends now."

I feel kind of silly for being scared of Graff just because of how he looks. I clear my throat and say, "We call him Pockets. You know, because of all his pockets?"

Graff grins again. "Makes sense to me. C'mon, Pockets, let's get you cleaned up." He leads a complaining Pockets over to the other end of the room and pushes him through some curtains. We hear the *whoosh* of water, and then some bubbles spill out from under the curtain. A minute later the whirr of a dryer drowns out the sound of the mechanics working. Then out runs Pockets, clean and mostly dry. His fur doesn't look any shorter, though.

Dad looks Pockets up and down. "Couldn't you have given him a haircut while you were at it?"

Graff laughs. "I wouldn't put pointy

scissors anywhere near that cat. He's quicker than he looks."

Pockets twists his head around to admire himself. "Better," he admits. "Now we really need to get the taxi aqua-fitted. Nautilus will surely have lost more water since we left Earth."

"Already taken care of." Graff steps aside to reveal our taxi, parked right behind us. While we were waiting for Pockets to get clean, the other guys must have been working on the car. Can't say that it looks any different, though.

"Wonderful," Dad says, circling the taxi. He must see something I don't.

"You are now able to go underwater," Graff says proudly.

"How deep?" Pockets asks.

Graff rubs his chin. More grease squirts

out. "We're not sure. At some point the pressure of the water will begin to crush the taxi."

"When is that?" Dad asks. "At fifty yards down? Five hundred?"

Graff shrugs. "Somewhere between those two?"

Pockets sighs. "Okay. So what else can it do?"

"Push the blue button on the dashboard. Skis will pop out of the bottom for a water landing," Graff says.

"Nice," Dad says, nodding.

Graff reaches into the backseat of the taxi and hands Pockets a brown bag. "The ISF also requested you stock up on a few things. We packed you a heat sensor and a few other tools."

Pockets peeks into the bag. "A Flirbin Blaster. Excellent."

"What's a Flirbin Blaster?" I ask, leaning over to look.

Pockets closes the bag. "Sorry, that's on a need-to-know basis only."

"Hmph," I reply.

Graff puts his hand on my shoulder, depositing three circles of grease. "Don't feel too bad, young Morningstar. Here, you can have a gadget of your own." He reaches into his tool belt and hands me what looks like a flashlight with a suction cup at the end. I turn it over in my hands. "What is it?"

"It's called an air dryer."

"A hair dryer?" I say, trying to hide my disappointment. I have one of those at home. Mom usually has to chase me around the apartment before I let her use it on me after a shower.

He laughs. "No, an *air* dryer. We use it to make repairs underwater. It allows us to pull out objects that get stuck in a drain line. Seeing as you're already in your swimsuit, I figured this is something you might like."

"Are you sure he should take this?" Dad asks. "It looks expensive."

"No worries," Graff says. "We've got plenty of 'em."

"Thanks!" I tell him, gripping it tight. A gadget of my very own! And it won't dry my hair!

Graff gives Pockets a little scratch on the top of his head and says, "Be well, my friend."

If anyone had told me a week ago that it would seem normal that a giant ant-like creature would be lovingly petting an oversize talking cat, I'd have told them they were nuts. Welcome to life in outer space!

Pockets is in a hurry to get to the water planet, but not in enough of a hurry to miss out on tuna at Barney's Bagels and Schmear. Dad tries to convince him we should get moving, but he pretends not to hear. We have no choice but to go with him. Truth be told, a bagel really does sound good.

Pockets plunks his money on the counter. "Three tuna bagel sandwiches," he says. "Heavy on the tuna."

"I was actually going to get cream cheese on mine," I tell Pockets.

"Oh, I wasn't ordering for you," he replies, licking his lips. "These are all for me."

Dad orders for the two of us and I follow

Pockets to a table. He digs into his lunch while I look around, trying to find the differences between this Barney's and the one not too far from our apartment on Earth.

For one thing, ours doesn't have a view of the Milky Way outside its window. And the guy behind the counter at home doesn't have six tentacles or three eyes. Or if he does, he did a really great job hiding it that one time I saw him. This Barney's is packed, just like the bagel shop at home. Only this one is full of aliens of all shapes and sizes and colors. Dad joins us and catches me staring. He gives me a disapproving look. I turn my attention to my food. Who could blame me if I peek every few seconds at a square-shaped alien at the next table? His mouth opens so wide he can (and does) stuff his whole sandwich in it.

"Is this seat taken?" a small voice asks.

I turn around to see a tiny red alien with one large eye in the center of his round face. Two long tentacles sway back and forth on the top of his head, like windshield wipers. He's holding a tray of food, and for some reason he looks kind of familiar. He clears his throat and asks again if the seat is taken.

"No," Dad and I say, quickly scooting down on the bench to make room.

"Yes," Pockets says, barely glancing up from his sandwich. "Sorry."

The alien's little tentacles droop and he hurries away, bent over his tray.

"That was rude, Pockets," Dad says. "There's plenty of room."

"And he was so cute," I add. "Like a little stuffed animal, but real."

Pockets licks the last bits of tuna off his paws and stands up. "Trust me, looks can be deceiving out here."

I try to see where the little red guy went, but I don't spot him anywhere in the restaurant. I could stay here all day just alien watching, but now that Pockets has eaten his tuna, he hurries us out.

Graff gassed up the taxi earlier, so we are soon zooming away from Akbar's Floating Rest Stop. According to my map, the only tricky part of the rest of the journey should be avoiding an asteroid that is very close to Nautilus. The big chunk of floating rock is only fifty miles across, which isn't big enough to give it much gravitational pull. So it shouldn't pull us toward it, but it can definitely crush us if we hit it. Or it hits us. Either way, it would be bad.

It doesn't take long until we enter the water planet's solar system. Just like the map warned, the asteroid is here. We are all silent as the huge chunk of space rock zooms by the taxi's rear window a little too close for comfort. The taxi bumps and jumps for a minute in the wake of the asteroid, then settles back down.

Soon we've reached the planet's atmosphere. "Deploy reverse thrusters," I tell Dad.

"Roger that," he says. But before he gets a chance, a huge, gushing wall of water appears out of nowhere and blocks our way.

That was definitely NOT on my map!

CHAPTER FIVE:
The Underwater Planet

"It's the water leaving Nautilus," Pockets shouts above the roar. "You will have to go above it."

"I can't," Dad shouts back, swerving left, then right. "The gravity from the planet is too strong at this point. It's pulling us toward it."

Then, just as suddenly as it appeared, the huge spout of water is gone. A few large drops splash against our windshield, and then all is quiet.

"That was weird," I say when my heart stops pounding. "Why is the water doing that?"

"That's what we're here to find out," Pockets says, almost cheerfully. He likes mysteries, too.

A thick, dark cloud hovers over most of Nautilus. It's not until the taxi flies below it that I can see why they call Nautilus a water planet.

Almost the entire surface is covered in water. I've never been to the ocean on Earth before, but this must be what it's like, only times a *hundred*. The water is an amazing light green color. I wonder what it would be like to swim in it! I know we're here on a mission, but it would be a shame to let my bathing suit go to waste.

"How about that one, Archie?" Dad asks. He's pointing at a circle of tiny islands connected by long silver bridges.

I don't even need to look down at my map. "Sorry, Dad. None of the islands have runways nearly long enough to land on."

"I figured," Dad says, gritting his teeth. "Let's hope this new landing gear works." He presses the new blue button on the dashboard. We wait. I don't hear anything.

"Did the skis come out underneath?" I ask, pressing my face up to my window.

Pockets scrambles to the other window. "I don't see anything," he reports.

"And there's no time to deploy my hot-air balloon."

I twist around. "You have a hot-air balloon?"

"Actually, I have two," he says. "I'll show you someday. Unless of course the taxi is smashed to bits when it hits the water. Then you'll just have to take my word for it."

I gulp.

"Hang on, boys, here we go," Dad says as the front of the taxi becomes level with the planet. He grips the steering wheel so tight his knuckles turn white. I hold my breath as the taxi skims across the surface of the water. We wobble back and forth, with first the front and then the back of the cab dipping underneath the water. Finally the taxi steadies itself and we start gently floating on the ripples toward the group of islands.

"Phew," Dad says, unpeeling his fingers from the wheel.

"Phew," Pockets and I agree.

"Wow, look!" I shout, rolling down my window. The water is so clear that I can see straight down to the ocean floor. I see round buildings and long sidewalks and so many people! Some are walking—more like gliding, really—while most are swimming. Some are even riding three-wheeled bicycles on the ocean floor.

"Wow," Pockets says, going from window to window in the backseat to get the best view.

"Wow," Dad agrees, sticking his head out his own window.

A group of people wave from a dock on the largest island. They rush to meet us as we pull in. Tall and thin, with fins instead of hands, they look more like fish than people. I'm not scared of them, though, like I was of Graff at first. After all, unlike the ants in kindergarten, Mom's never had to pull *fish* from my hair. That would be really, really gross.

They use a rope to tie us to the dock, then help us out of the car. Pockets flips open his official ISF badge and then introduces Dad and me.

"We are so glad you're here," a fish-person in a long blue robe with wide sleeves says. He bends way down to shake our hands. His fin-like hand is cold and clammy, but not in a bad way.

"I am Carp," he says. "I am the leader of the undersea people."

A woman in a green robe steps up next to him and shakes our hands, too. Her hand is much warmer, and a bit less fin-like. "And I am Salmon," she says, "leader of the abovesea people."

Carp turns to Pockets and says, "Salmon and I will fill you in on our current situation. Meanwhile, my son, Pike, will be happy to entertain the earthlings with a tour."

"Oh, I get it," I say with a grin. "Everyone here is named after a fish!"

"What do you mean?" Carp asks.

Pockets gives me a quick shake of his head.

"Never mind," I mutter, my cheeks growing hot.

Pike steps out from behind his father. He's like a mini version of his dad. I guess I must look like a mini version of *my* dad, too.

I lean over and whisper to Dad, "Shouldn't we stay with Pockets? How can we help him if we're not together?"

"He'll let us know if he needs us," Dad replies.

Pockets turns and motions for us to go with Pike. He and the two leaders hurry toward a nearby table.

"Come," Pike says, grabbing my hand in his cold one. "Let's go have fun!" He pulls me away from the dock and onto a grassy area. Dad glances back at our taxi bobbing in the water, seems satisfied that it's safe, and follows.

Pike points out the houses in the center

of the island. They look like they are made of dried-out mud. Colorful flowers and plants bloom everywhere and make the homes look cozy and inviting.

"Why do some people live up here, and some in the water?" I ask Pike.

"We all used to live undersea," he explains, climbing onto a large pile of moss-covered rocks. Dad and I step where he steps, being careful not to slip.

When we reach the top, he continues his story. "A few hundred years ago, people started exploring above. And now it has become home to many. If the oceans continue to dry up, then everyone will have to live above the water. Most of our bodies are not prepared for that. We do not breathe air well enough to live here full-time."

He kind of sounds like Pockets when he talks—all grown-up, even though he's still a kid. But then he suddenly does a backflip, stretches out his fin-like arms, and shouts, "Long live Nautilus!" No way Pockets would—or could—do *that*. Not that I could do it, either. I can't even do a somersault.

I clap and Pike grins, puffing out the gills on his cheeks.

"Very impressive," Dad says.

"One day I will be leader of the undersea," Pike says. "If there is an undersea left, that is. You are not visiting us at our best time." He points up at the huge cloud we flew past on our way here. It blocks most of the sun. "That cloud began to form when the water started disappearing," he says. "Usually our planet is sunny and warm."

"What do you think is making the water go away?" I ask.

His eyes dim. "Some undersea people think the abovesea people are behind it."

"But why would they want to get rid of the water?"

The gills on his face flap as he frowns. "If the water goes away, then everything undersea will be abovesea. Instead of only having a few islands to live on, they'll have the whole planet." His eyes get wet with tears. "And the rest of us won't be able to breathe."

"Do you really think they'd do that?" I ask. "Salmon seemed really nice. She's the leader of the abovesea people, right?"

Pike nods. "I don't really think they would do it. Neither does my father. But that's why the ISF officer is here, to help figure it out." He grins. "Come, let's forget our troubles for a moment. I want to show you my favorite place abovesea."

He leads us down the other side of the rocks and around to a hidden sandy cove. Two fish-men in uniforms sit on lifeguard stands on either side of the small beach.

"Do the lifeguards mean we can swim here?" I ask as we make our way toward the water. I spread my arms to show off my swimsuit. "I came prepared."

Pike laughs but shakes his head. "I'm sorry. But until we figure out what's happening with the water, swimming up here on the surface has been banned. And these men aren't lifeguards. They are guarding the entrance to the Nautilus National Bank below us."

One of the guards leans back in his chair and closes his eyes. The other pulls out a book to read.

"The bank hasn't been robbed in fifty years," Pike explains. "So they're pretty bored. People don't last too long at this job. These guys have only been here a few—"

A roaring *whoosh* drowns out the rest of his words. A steady stream of water races from the ocean right up to the sky, like an upside-down waterfall. The force of it pushes me and Pike backward onto the beach, but Dad is standing by the shore-line and falls the other way, right into the shallow water! By the time we scramble to our feet and reach him, the huge plume of water has disappeared, leaving the ocean as calm as ever.

Dad sits upright in the wet sand, water lapping at his waist.

"Are you all right, Mr. Morningstar?" Pike asks, bending down.

Dad looks up at us. Surprise and delight

shine on his face. "This is the most refreshing water I've ever felt!" he says. Then he looks down at his wrist. "Oops, I got my watch wet." He peers closer at it. "Hey, it still works!"

Pike nods. "Our water is truly something special."

I am TOTALLY wishing I'd fallen in, too. I could slip while helping Dad stand up. Accidentally, of course. Then if I splashed around while trying to get out, that wouldn't be considered swimming, right? I'm about to put my plan into action, when Pockets comes running onto the beach, followed by a breathless Salmon and Carp.

"We must get back to the taxi!" Pockets shouts. "The bank has just been robbed!"

Chapter Six

Under the Sea

We race back to the dock and pile into the taxi. "Follow us," Salmon says. She and Carp and Pike dive below the clear surface.

"Let's see what this baby can do underwater," Dad says, flicking a switch on the dashboard. I hold on tight as the sides of the taxi stretch out while the front flattens into the shape of a duck's bill. Instead of the rocket boosters that normally come out of the back of the taxi when we take off, propellers pop up and push the taxi down through the water. The wings move up and down now, like fins!

"That Graff does fine work," Dad says, leaning back in his seat as we go deeper.

"He does indeed," Pocket agrees. "But I am fairly certain *that's* not supposed to happen." He points to the rear window behind him. A thin crack has started to form down the middle.

Dad gulps loudly. "If the water pressure gets much stronger," he warns, "that window will break and the car could spin out of control."

My eyes widen. That doesn't sound good. Meanwhile, we keep going lower and the crack keeps growing. "We'd better warn the others," Dad says.

I look all around but don't see anyone. "The bubbles from the propellers are blocking them," I tell Dad.

"Hopefully, they are safely out of the way," he replies. "Graff warned us he didn't know how deep we could go before the water pressure would crush the car. I wish we knew how far we are from the ocean floor."

Pockets taps his paw against his chin, deep in thought. Then he says, "If only we had a copilot with a map to guide our way underwater..."

Yeah, that *would* be helpful. Oh, wait!

He means me! I quickly grab my map and pull it out of its tube. I'm not sure it will show us what's under the water, but it's worth a try.

It works! Instead of suns and planets and wormholes popping up in the air in front of me, I can see tunnels and buildings not too far below us, and reefs made of jagged rock and sand. Speaking of reefs! "Turn right, Dad!" I shout. "Reef wall directly in front of us!"

Dad veers quickly to the right. The edge of the left propeller clips the reef, but it doesn't look too serious. We're still in one piece.

"Good timing, Archie," he says when we level out. He shuts off the propellers and I glance behind us at the rear window, fearing the worst. But the crack doesn't look any worse. In fact, it looks...better? I'm about to ask how that's possible, when I see Pockets slip a tube of something into a pocket.

"Super-extra-special ISF glue," he says when he sees me looking.

"You could have mentioned you had that," I reply.

"I could have," Pockets admits. "But you need to learn how to handle dangerous situations. That's what will make you a better ISF deputy."

I'm about to argue that we are supposed to be a team, but I really *do* want to be the best deputy I can be. So I mutter something that would probably get me in trouble if anyone heard, and I turn back around. Without the bubbles from the propellers, I easily spot Carp and Salmon swimming up ahead. Pike swims up to my window, worry all over his face. He must have seen our near miss with the reef wall.

I give him a thumbs-up.

"There it is," Pockets says. "The Nautilus National Bank." We glide toward a huge white building with a silver dome on the top. Carp and Salmon wave us into an open garage.

A metal door lowers and seals us in. The water level in the garage slowly gets lower and lower as the water is sucked down a big drain on the floor. When only puddles are left on the floor, we open the doors.

Pockets hops out first, a huge grin on his face. "Guess what?" he asks.

"We made it without being crushed or crashing?" I say.

"Well, yes, that," he says. "But guess who's underwater without a drop of water on him? Me!" He beams with delight.

I shake my head. That cat *really* doesn't like water.

A door swings open at the far end of the garage. Pike runs through it to greet us. "I am so glad you made it safely, Archie," he says. "That looked pretty scary."

"It was the taxi's first time underwater," I admit. "But the three of us are a good team."

Dad pats me on the shoulder as we all walk into the bank. Broken tiles and bricks lie in piles on the floor, but other than that, the bank looks pretty much like a regular bank. Lots of thick marble walls, shiny floors, and big doors with big locks.

Carp hurries up to Pockets and says, "It appears the alarm went off before the robbers could complete the tunnel they were digging. We don't yet know whether anything was stolen or not. The abovesea people are blaming the undersea people, and the undersea people are blaming those above. Salmon is trying to keep the peace, but it's a mess!"

Pockets pulls out a yellow pencil from a small pocket under his arm. "Never fear," he says. "The ISF is here."

I'm about to tell Pockets he made a rhyme, but he's in his official ISF officer mode and probably wouldn't appreciate the teasing right now.

I figure he's going to pull out a notebook next, but he doesn't. Instead he presses down on the pencil's eraser and the biggest magnifying glass I've ever seen pops out. He holds it up in front of his face. Pike and I laugh. "You should see how big your nose looks!" I tell him.

"And your whiskers!" Pike adds.

Pockets moves the magnifying glass forward and back so his nose gets really big and long. Pike and I crack up. Then Pockets glances at Carp and quickly puts his serious expression back on. "This will help me find any clues the robbers left behind," he explains to everyone. "And they always leave clues behind."

"You'll need to start outside," Carp says. "Before any evidence gets washed away."

"Outside?" Pockets asks. His eyes begin to dart around the room, like he's looking for an escape. "Outside in the *water*, you mean?"

"Of course," Carp says. "The robbers broke in from outside. Any clues would be there. If we're not too late already."

Pockets is clearly frozen with fear. I'm not even sure he's breathing. Only his eyes are moving. I've never seen him look like this. I'm not sure what to do. Suddenly I *do* know. We're a team. Sure, Pockets is the leader when we're on missions, but we help each other out. I step forward. "I'll go," I tell Carp. "You need Pockets here on the inside. Someone has to keep the peace between the two sides. He's really good at that."

Carp looks unsure, but then Dad steps forward. "I'll go, too," he offers. "Four eyes are better than two."

"Make that *six* eyes," Pike says, joining us. "They'll need someone to show them around."

Carp nods. "Fine. Let's get moving."

Pockets finally takes a breath. He reaches out to squeeze my hand with his paw. Then he whips out what look like plastic fishbowls and hands one to me and one to Dad. "These helmets will let you breathe underwater for a half hour," he explains.

Dad and I slip the helmets over our

heads. They instantly seal around our shoulders. Cool!

Pockets pulls us into a huddle, including Pike. "Keep your eyes open for anything unusual," he says.

"How will we know what's unusual?" I ask. "There's a city under the ocean. Everything is unusual."

Pockets considers this. "Good point. Each crime scene is different, of course, but one rule is always the same: You need to look for something that seems out of place, like it doesn't belong there."

Pockets looks from me to Dad. "This is good practice for Intergalactic Security Force deputies." He pats us on the back and hurries off with his huge magnifying glass pencil.

"You'll get to see how we keep the bank dry," Pike says. "It's pretty cool." He leads Dad and me to a nearby hole in the wall. I'd thought this was part of the damage from the robbery, but clearly it's meant to be here. It's dry when we step inside it, but it slopes downward, slowly filling with water until we can swim right out.

"Definitely cool," I agree, spreading my arms and lifting off the ground.

Dad was right—this water is amazing. It's almost crackling with energy. It feels thicker than the water at home, almost like I'm swimming through syrup. No... it's not really sticky like that, more like pudding. Penny would love it, since she loves anything to do with pudding. Suddenly,

Penny and Mom feel really far away and I get a pang of homesickness. Then I remind myself that I'm getting to swim deep underwater on another planet and I know Mom would want me to enjoy it.

I follow Pike around to the back of the bank, where we spot a huge hole almost as big as the bank itself. Piled on all sides of the hole are equally huge mounds of sand mixed with shiny black rocks that must have come out of the ocean floor.

Dad motions that he'll take a closer look on one side and I should take the other. I swim around to the smallest pile and start looking. Mostly I see sand. A lot of sand and a lot of rocks. The shiny rocks are very pretty. I reach for one the size of a golf ball and try to pull it off the pile to bring home for Penny. Only it won't come off. I try a different one. It moves a little but snaps right back into place. They're all stuck to one another, like magnets!

I'm about to give up, when I remember the air-dryer gadget Graff gave me back

at the garage. I pull it out of the pocket of my swim shorts and push the end with the suction cup against the pile of rocks. One flick of a switch later and a small rock bursts free of the pile and shoots inside the tube. A little cover slides over the top, sealing it in.

I grin. That was easy! I try to slide the gadget back into my pocket, but it misses and drops slowly to the ocean floor. When I bend to pick it up, a small metal object in the sand catches my eye. It's a screwdriver! My first clue as an ISF deputy! What a rush!

My heart beating fast, I grab it with both hands.

Only I can't make it budge at all. I wave my arms in the water and call out, "Guys!

Come see what I found!" I'm not sure they can hear me through the fishbowl on my head, but my splashing around gets their attention. I grab hold of the tool while Dad and Pike tug on my arms. It takes all three of us yanking REALLY HARD to pull it free from the large rocks. I open up the air dryer and drop the screwdriver inside to keep it safe. As I tighten the cap, I realize I could have used it to pull the screwdriver free from the magnetized rocks. Oops!

We keep searching the area but don't see anything else out of the ordinary. Dad points to his helmet and then to his watch. We're almost out of breathing time.

We swim back through the tunnel until swimming turns to walking and we're inside again. We yank off our helmets and hurry over to Pockets and Carp. I unscrew the top of my air dryer and flip it over while Dad describes the huge hole.

The small rock falls out into my palm first, followed by the screwdriver, which is stuck to the end of the rock. "Could this be something?" I ask, prying them apart and handing Pockets the tool.

Pockets holds his giant magnifying glass up to it and lets out a sharp meow. "It sure is something!" he shouts, pointing to the edge. With the magnifying glass we can clearly read the words PROPERTY OF B.U.R.P.

B.U.R.P.? The biggest, baddest group of criminals in the universe is involved in this? I'm so surprised that I drop the black rock. It clatters noisily to the marble floor.

Two things happen really fast after that. Pockets shouts, "Whoa!" and the screwdriver flies out of his paw, over Pike's head, and into my hand.

Chapter Seven:
A Postcard Would've Been Nice

"What just happened?" Dad asks as I struggle to peel the screwdriver from my palm. It takes some effort, but finally I'm able to push it into Pockets's paw. He grasps it tight this time.

"It was the stone," Carp says. "It is not supposed to reach the air."

The rock has rolled between Dad's feet. "This little rock?" he asks, bending over to pick it up.

"Don't!" Carp says, stepping between Dad and the rock. "Over the centuries the people of Nautilus have adapted to the strongly magnetic mineral that is found under our ocean floor. It has no effect on us. But when visitors to our planet come in contact with it when the stone is dry, *they* become magnetic."

Dad backs away from the rock and pulls me close to him. "Is it dangerous?" he asks, his voice tight.

Carp shakes his head. "He only touched it with one hand. He'll be fine in a few days. A few weeks at most."

"I'm sorry, Dad," I say. "I thought it would be a cool gift for Penny."

He sighs. "Maybe next time just get her a postcard."

Pockets pulls a square coin out of his pocket and tosses it at me. It lands right in the palm of my hand without me even reaching for it. Cool! I peel the alien coin off my hand and slip it in my pocket.

I'm not sure I mind being magnetic if it means I get to pick up stray coins from different planets. I might even start a collection!

"Hey!" Pockets says. His tail starts swishing back and forth like windshield wipers.

"Okay, okay," I say, reaching into my pocket for the coin. "I'll give it back."

"No, it's not that," Pockets says quickly. "I've just realized I know what B.U.R.P. was doing down here. And they weren't robbing the bank."

"Sure looks like it," Carp says.

Pockets shakes his head. "I believe they want what is buried under the ocean floor—the rocks! And judging by the size of the hole, they want a LOT of them.

The digging must have set off the bank alarms."

"If that's true," Salmon says, "then where are all the rocks? There's nowhere to hide them."

I look down at my small rock, still lying on the floor. If I hadn't taken it, I wouldn't have found the screwdriver, and Pockets wouldn't have figured out what B.U.R.P. was after. Strange how one thing leads to another. Suddenly, the pieces come together like a puzzle. "It's the water," I blurt out.

"*What's* the water, Archie?" Dad asks.

"That's how they're getting the mineral off the planet," I explain. "It's like when me and Penny play at the pool, you know, with that water jet, and it's so strong it pushes our hands away? Couldn't those really powerful gushes of water be bringing the rocks up to the sky?"

Pockets claps his paws together. "The boy is absolutely right! B.U.R.P. has been grinding up the rocks and then setting off the waterspouts to send the magnetic material right up to the sky. It's a brilliant plot!"

Carp and Salmon stare with wide eyes at Pockets, then turn to face each other. "I am so ashamed," Carp says. "We were blaming each other when it was B.U.R.P. taking our water all along."

"Not our finest moment," Salmon agrees. "I am sorry, too."

The two leaders shake hands warmly.

"And the good news is that the water

and the rocks are still here," Pockets says, "inside that huge cloud. They haven't gotten away with it."

Pike rushes in from the other room. "Everyone! Come quick! The cloud is moving!"

Chapter Eight:
A Sticky Situation

Between me worrying about avoiding the reef wall and Pockets worrying about being too late to catch B.U.R.P., the ride up to the surface is not much fun. We finally reach the dock and scramble out of the taxi. I shiver. The cloud is even bigger now, after the last spout, and it completely blocks the sun.

Abovesea and undersea people huddle together on the island. Many are looking up at the huge cloud, but others are still talking about the bank robbery. The two guards we saw earlier at the beach are trying to keep everyone calm, but it doesn't seem to be working very well.

The cloud is moving slowly, but it's definitely moving. It also seems to have started humming. That's not something you usually hear from clouds. In fact, you usually don't hear *anything* from clouds. I mean, except for thunder, of course. But thunder doesn't hum. At least it doesn't on Earth.

"Does the cloud usually hum?" I ask Pike.

"I've never heard that sound before," he says, moving noticeably closer to his dad.

Pockets whips out a pair of the biggest binoculars I've ever seen.

"It's the engines of a spaceship!" he declares. "It's pulling the cloud!"

The crowd gasps.

"Are we going after it?" I ask, already plotting out the route in my head.

He shakes his head. "By the time we got up there, whoever is in that ship would be on the other side of the galaxy. I have a better idea." He stashes the binoculars away and pulls out a long gold-colored tube. It looks a little like the tube I stash my space map in, only this one is wider and longer and not black with a silver star on it. He holds it up. "My trusty new Flirbin Blaster is going to fix things right up."

I'm about to ask what it does, but Pockets is busy fishing around for something else. He finally pulls out a rain poncho. In one motion, he slips it over his head. Then he aims the Flirbin Blaster at the cloud and twists the bottom. Instantly, a stream of something white shoots straight into the sky. Little bits of it waft down onto my back and neck. "Ow, that's COLD!" I begin to shiver.

"The Flirbin Blaster shoots dry ice," Pockets explains. He keeps it aimed at the cloud.

"Dry ice?" I repeat. "Like what the doctor uses to burn off a wart?" I personally haven't had experience with this, but Dad's always coming home from work with weird things on his body. He must be

picking up germs from the planets he visits on his route. I have a feeling I'm going to be taking a lot more baths from now on.

"Well, yes," Pockets says impatiently. "I suppose you could use it for wart removal."

"And it looks cool at parties," Dad adds. "Like you're dancing on a fluffy white cloud."

"But how will it help us now?" I ask, having trouble picturing my dad dancing on a regular floor, let alone a cloud.

Instead of answering, Pockets tosses ponchos to Dad and me. "Quick, put these on. Make sure you are completely covered."

No sooner do I flip up my hood and thrust my hands into the pockets than it begins to rain. Slowly at first, and then the drops fall faster and faster until everyone around us is soaked. Tiny fragments of black rock stick to my poncho, like pulp in fresh-squeezed orange juice.

Finally the rain stops, and for the first time since we've been on Nautilus, the sun comes out, and with it, the heat. Pockets wiggles out of his poncho and tosses it aside. I notice he's careful not to touch the outside. Dad and I do the same.

"Where'd the spaceship go?" Pike asks, shielding his eyes as he searches the sky.

Carp frowns. "Now we will never know how they were able to get into our oceans without anyone seeing them. As you can tell by looking at us, someone from another planet would certainly stand out."

"Unless they wore disguises so that they could blend in," Pockets says, grinning.

He rushes over to the crowd. We all share a puzzled look but hurry after him.

There's some big commotion in the center of the group. Pockets pushes his way through and then announces, "Aha! Gotcha!" He does a backflip right over a picnic bench (guess I was wrong about him being able to do that!) and tackles two men to the ground. I stare down in surprise as I recognize the uniforms the men are wearing.

"No, Pockets," I shout. "Those are the guards from the beach. They're not from B.U.R.P."

"Really?" Pockets asks. "Then explain *this*." He flips both the men over (truly, he is very strong for a cat), and we all gasp. Up close, I can see that the guards' hands are plastic gloves painted to *look* like real fins! These men aren't from Nautilus at all! Every spot that isn't covered by their uniforms is covered in something metal. Coins, spoons, keys, paper clips.

One of the guards even has a frying pan stuck to his arm!

I look back up at Pockets, who is standing over the magnetized guards, grinning proudly. I realize now that this was part of his plan all along. Making it rain would not only return the water and the mineral to Nautilus—it would reveal the bad guys as soon as the mineral dried on their skin. That Pockets is one smart cat!

The guards try to stand up, but Salmon and Carp spring into action and hold them firmly in place.

Pockets holds up his badge. "I am Intergalactic Security Force officer Pilarbing Fangorious Catapolitus," he tells the guards. "Otherwise known as Pockets." He winks at me before turning back to the guards. "You are under arrest for helping B.U.R.P. steal minerals from beneath the ocean floor of the planet Nautilus."

Before the guards can argue, Pockets's badge flies out of his hand and sticks to one of the guard's cheeks. Pockets leans over and peels it off. "I'll take that back, thank you very much."

The guards grumble angrily. I quietly unstick a paper clip from my hand. No need to remind everyone that I have something in common with the criminals.

"Looks like your friend up there has ditched you," Pockets tells them, waving at the sky. "But the ISF will be happy to give you a ride off the planet. Your plan to steal the mineral is foiled."

One of the guards grunts. "The mineral

was just the start," he says. "We were going to make a giant magnet and drag the asteroid away."

The other guard kicks his friend in the shin. "Don't tell them anything!"

Dad and I look at each other in surprise. The *asteroid*? The one we dodged on the way here? Pockets must be surprised, too, but he doesn't show it. In a flash, he has both guards handcuffed and tied together.

"B.U.R.P. will find another way to steal an asteroid—just you wait," the first guard snarls, trying unsuccessfully to pull at the knots around his arms. The second guard goes to kick him again and the metal tip of his boot gets stuck to the first guard's knee.

It's hard not to laugh.

Salmon and a bunch of other abovesea

people form a circle around the guards while Carp and Pike walk us to our taxi.

"What do you think they were planning to do with the asteroid?" Pike asks Pockets. He's been staring at him in awe ever since Pockets single-handedly took down the criminals.

Pockets thinks for a moment. "If they could control an asteroid, they could do a lot of damage to any planet in their path."

"An asteroid landing on my planet wiped out all the dinosaurs," I tell Pike. "And the dinosaurs were REALLY big and had been there for a long time."

"Let's hope B.U.R.P. gave up their plans," Carp says, putting his hand on his son's shoulder. To the rest of us he says, "We can't thank you enough for all you've done. After the rain, the ocean is back to its normal level now. And just as important, our people are again united."

Pockets tips an imaginary hat at them. "Just doing my job," he says. Then he puts his paws around me and Dad and adds, "We're just doing *our* job, I mean."

Pockets climbs into the backseat first, springing easily over the gap between the dock and the taxi. He reaches into a pocket and pulls out his pillow and what looks like an ordinary sheet. But when he pulls it over himself, he completely blends into the seat! Other than a vague cat-shaped spot, I can't see him at all. Pike and I gasp.

"How are you doing that?" I ask.

"It's my camouflage blanket," he explains. "A very handy gadget for when I want to hide in plain sight. Or when I don't want to be bothered. It's been way too long since my last nap." And with that, he begins to snore.

Dad and I climb into the taxi a lot less gracefully than Pockets did. I don't need to bother to reach for the seat belt, since the end of it instantly flies into my hand. I have to pry it off in order to click it in place. I'm going to have to dig out my winter gloves when I get home, or the kids at school are gonna start asking questions when their lunch money flies out of their hands and sticks to mine! Although, then they'll think it's weird that I'm wearing gloves in school. Oh, well. No one said being an ISF deputy was going to be easy.

Pike stands at my door. "It was wonderful to meet you, Archie," he says. "I will never forget you."

"Me, either," I tell him. "Even after my hand returns to normal."

He laughs and waves good-bye. Then he walks to the edge of the dock and does a perfect dive into the ocean.

"I wish I could do that," I tell Dad.

"Maybe one day Pike will teach you," Dad replies, checking his mirrors.

"Really? Do you think I'll see him again?"

"It's possible, Archie. The universe may be a very big place, but good friends make it a lot smaller."

Dad twists the com line on. "Morningstar and son, setting a course for home."

"Is the cat with you?" the mouse asks.

Dad glances in the backseat. "Well, can't say as I see him right now. He sort of disappeared." Dad winks at me and I stifle a laugh.

"Just like a cat," the mouse scoffs. "Can't be trusted, I tell you."

Pockets growls.

"I thought you were asleep," I call back to him.

"I am," Pockets replies.

"Who is that?" the mouse asks. "Is that the cat? I told you he can't be—"

Dad and I laugh while Pockets hisses. "Morningstar out," Dad says, switching off the line. The taxi's engine roars to life, and we are on our way home.

I twist around in my seat one last time. Pike gives one final wave and then dives beneath the water's surface. I sit back and smile. The universe just became a little smaller.

THREE SCIENCE FACTS TO IMPRESS YOUR FRIENDS AND TEACHERS

1. Where do **CLOUDS** come from? When the sun warms up the air, water from oceans and lakes and rivers begins to evaporate. This means it turns into water vapor (a gas that you can't see) and begins to rise through the air. As the air gets cooler, the vapor sticks to dust in the atmosphere. Eventually the rising water vapor comes together to form a cloud. When the cloud grows heavy with water droplets and it can't hold any more, the water falls from the clouds and it begins to rain. Fog is a cloud that has formed at ground level.

2. A SUBMARINE (called a sub for short) is a large vessel that travels underwater. It is large enough for a crew of people to live inside it. Scientists use subs to explore beneath the ocean, and the navy uses them to help keep the oceans safe. Some can go as deep as eight hundred feet. A sub is also a kind of sandwich, but it would get very soggy underwater and no one would want to eat it. Except for Pockets, if it were a tuna sub.

3. MAGNETITE is a mineral found underground in parts of the world. This is where the word for *magnet* comes from. Magnets can push and pull on things with an invisible force by creating what is called a magnetic field. The magnetic field attracts certain metals like iron, nickel, and cobalt. Anything made out of these materials will stick to something magnetic.

By Wendy Mass and Michael Brawer

ⓁⒷ

LITTLE, BROWN AND COMPANY
New York   Boston

For Bethany, who lovingly guides our little taxi through the cosmos.

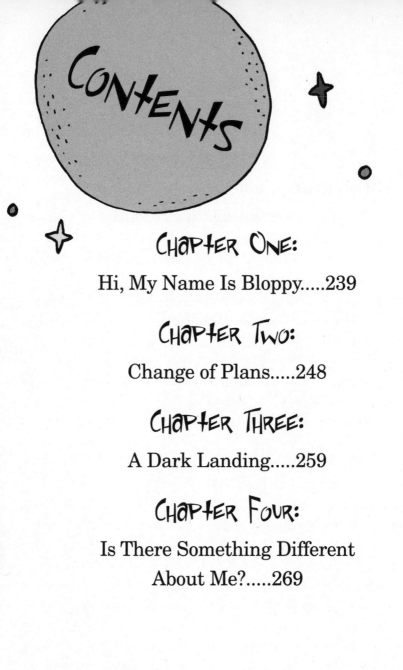

CONTENTS

Chapter One:
Hi, My Name Is Bloppy

If you've never been woken up by your little sister lifting your eyelid with sticky peanut butter fingers, consider yourself lucky.

It's still dark, so it can't be time to wake up for school yet. Plus, it's Saturday. I try to bat Penny's hand away, but she grabs my sleeve and tugs. I groan. "Can't you see I'm sleeping?" She doesn't answer, of course. It's times like this when I wish Penny would say more than two words in a row.

"Go back to sleep, Penny."

She tugs again. I rub my eyes and look at the clock. It's 11:55 at night. I start to lie back down when it hits me.

It's 11:55 at night!

My dad and I leave in five minutes and I'm still in my pajamas! The business of ridding the universe of supervillains has been slow these days, so Dad was allowed to get back to his regular space taxi job. I am still his awesome copilot. But not if I'm late! I throw off my blanket and, by mistake, Penny with it. Oops!

"Sorry!" I say, lifting her from the floor. She just giggles.

I look around for a pair of jeans. Yesterday's clothes *should* be in a heap by my bed. Ugh, Pockets cleaned my room again. I know he is bored not saving the universe every day, but he needs to find better ways to spend his time between missions.

"Why are you even awake?" I ask Penny as I grab clothes from my drawer.

She puffs out her pink cheeks. She does this when she's about to speak. The seconds tick by. I wait as patiently as an eight-year-old who is late for a trip into outer space can wait. Seriously, I should get some kind of award. Finally she blurts, "Kitty." Then she takes a deep breath and adds, "BIG kitty."

"Yes, he is a very big kitty," I agree, pulling a sweatshirt over my head. I should have figured Pockets woke her. He insists on sleeping at the end of her bed every night. Sometimes his purring wakes up the whole family. He purrs louder than Dad snores!

I lead Penny back into her room, and she climbs into bed. "Story?" she asks.

"Sorry," I whisper. "Bedtime stories are a Mommy thing."

She curls up around her stuffed purple dragon and is asleep before I shut the door. I tiptoe to the kitchen. Mom hands me my snack and thermos, my silver space map tube, and my Intergalactic Security Force badge. "Dad and Pockets are waiting for you in the car," she says, hugging me.

"Have fun. Make good choices." The fact that Mom doesn't seem nervous anymore when I go into space makes ME a little less nervous.

"Why is Pockets with us?" I ask Dad as we head downtown in the taxi. "Aren't we just picking up a regular customer?"

"Yup," Dad says, "but Pockets couldn't miss a chance at a tuna sandwich from Barney's."

Pockets springs up from his nap. "Did someone say tuna?" He rolls down his window, takes a deep whiff, and announces, "We have arrived!"

He bounds from the car before we come to a full stop in front of the restaurant. He's already eating by the time we get inside. The man behind the counter hands Dad a slip of paper and says, "Your pickup's in the back room."

I follow Dad to a door at the end of the restaurant. It's marked KEEP OUT.

"This is where the customers who can't blend in on Earth wait for their taxis," he explains. "You can open it."

But my hands stay at my sides. What if something gigantic is waiting on the other side, ready to shoot fire out of its eyes? "It says 'keep out,'" I tell him. "And you know how Mom's always telling me not to rush into things."

He laughs. "I promise it's okay."

I take a deep breath and face the door again. An ISF deputy has to be brave, I tell myself, and slowly push open the door. All I see at first is normal stuff that you'd find in the back room of a restaurant. Shelves with napkins, pickles, and ketchup, along with a few chairs set up in front of an old TV set. I relax. "I don't think our customer is back here, Dad."

Then out of the shadows glides the blobbiest, slimiest, gooiest creature I have ever seen. Picture a melting marshmallow snowman, only orange-colored like the inside of a ripe peach. He has two large black eyes, no visible nose, and a rectangle-shaped sticker on his chest that says HI, MY NAME IS BLOPPY.

I know it's not polite to stare, but wow. I've seen some odd-looking aliens in my short time as Dad's copilot, but nothing *this* odd. A puddle of orange goo lands at his feet. I watch as more goop drips and plops to the floor.

Dad looks down at the paper in his hand, clears his throat, and says, "Hi, Bloppy, I'm Sal Morningstar. My son and I will be taking you to Libra 6 today. Looks like it will be a one-way trip?"

Bloppy begins to quiver and shake. Maybe he's getting ready to shoot fire after all! I'm not proud of it, but I sort of hide behind Dad.

But no fire comes out of Bloppy—just big, wet, goopy tears.

Chapter Two:
Change of Plans

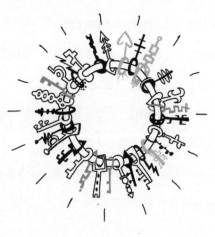

After about five minutes of crying and sniffling (turns out he DOES have a nose), Bloppy pulls himself together. "Sorry you had to see that," he says in a wobbly voice. "I'm starting a new job on Libra 6 tomorrow. I'm a little nervous."

"That's normal," Dad says, nodding. "I was nervous the first time I drove my taxi."

"And I was nervous the first time I had to be a copilot," I add. "I'm *still* nervous. But I love it. I bet you'll love your new job, too."

Bloppy shakes his head. "You two are lucky," he says sadly. "I know I won't like my new job selling shoes to ten-footed Orthopods, who have the smelliest feet in two galaxies, but I can't be picky. Not many choices out there for someone like me."

I guess most people don't want to hire you if you drip goop everywhere you go.

"I bet you'll feel better when we get there," Dad says. "We'll go out the back exit, and then I'll bring the taxi around."

It's a good thing Pockets has towels in

his awesome bottomless pockets. The way Bloppy is dripping, the backseat's gonna get awfully messy. But to my surprise, when we start moving to the door, all the goop on the floor slurps back up onto Bloppy's body! All that's left on the floor is a shiny glow.

That's a neat trick!

The door leads to a narrow alley, where the taxi is already waiting. Pockets jumps out of the driver's seat. Bloppy begins to quiver again.

"Cats can drive?" I ask, wide-eyed.

"Not all of them," Pockets replies. "As an ISF officer, I know how to drive more than three hundred different vehicles."

"Without the key?" Dad asks.

Pockets reaches into his fur and pulls out a huge silver circle with hundreds of keys dangling from it. "An ISF officer is always prepared."

Bloppy is now shaking all over and staring right at Pockets. Finally he shouts, "I LOVE cats!"

Before Pockets can duck, Bloppy has pulled him into a tight hug. I can barely see him—he almost completely disappears into the folds of Bloppy's blobs.

"Let me go!" Pockets shouts, but his voice is muffled, so it sounds like "Eat my toe!" Which I'm pretty sure is not what he means.

I reach over and tug on Bloppy's arm. It's less sticky than I thought it would be. "I don't think he can breathe," I tell him.

Bloppy lets go but stares adoringly. Pockets just glares. He's not the huggy type.

"Well," Dad says. "This is awkward."

"I'm sorry," Bloppy says. "On my home planet, cats are really friendly."

"Pockets is friendly," I tell Bloppy. "You just have to get to know him."

Dad opens the back door of the taxi. "Ready?" he asks.

Bloppy tries to climb in, but he's way too big to fit! Each time he squeezes one part of his body into the car, another part oozes out.

Dad and Pockets stand behind him and push. His head and belly make it in, but that's it. The rest hangs out the door. I run around to the other side of the car and grab his hands. I tug as hard as I can. My hands slide right out of his, and I fall back onto my butt.

"Are you all right, young human?" a concerned Bloppy asks from his half-in, half-out position. "Are you hurt?"

I dust myself off and reach back in. It's going to take more than *that* to keep an ISF deputy down! After another minute of pushing, pulling, and grunting, Bloppy fills every inch of the backseat. He smiles. "Whew!"

I return to my seat, exhausted, as Dad climbs into his. Pockets leans into my window. "And just where am I supposed to sit?" he asks.

I pat my knee. He sighs and climbs in. Settling on my lap, he says, "If you pet me, I'll bite."

I hold up my hands. "No petting, I promise."

Pockets sleeps through Bloppy's constant chattering about each cool thing we pass. *There are the moons of Jupiter! There goes a comet! Is that a new star?* He's fun to have along.

We're about halfway across the galaxy when the com system buzzes. "It must be Minerva calling back," Dad says. We had tried to check in with headquarters when we left, but a recorded message said Minerva was away from her desk. Dad turns the knob. "I was wondering when you'd check in, Minerva," Dad says. "We're on our way to Libra 6. Estimated time of arrival is—"

"Never mind that," a deep voice cuts him off. "You'll need to change course right away. You have a mission."

That's not Minerva's voice! I shake Pockets. "Wake up! Your dad is calling!"

Pockets jumps so high he lands on the ceiling of the car! He hangs from his claws, upside down. Bloppy and I gape at him. "That'd better not leave holes in the fabric," Dad warns.

"Father?" Pockets shouts. "Is everything all right?"

"Hello, son. I don't have time to tell you the whole story right now, so I'm beaming the information to your mini-tablet."

Pockets lands back on my lap with a thump. He reaches into a pocket and pulls out a small screen. I watch as text scrolls quickly across it.

"Morningstar!" Pockets's dad bellows.

I jump, but Dad remains calm. "Yes, Chief?" he says.

INCOMING MESSAGE...

"I'm sending the coordinates straight into your navigation system. My son will fill you in on the mission. This is an emergency, so you must drop your passenger off immediately. Good luck."

A second later my map begins to shake. It's never done *that* before! I have to hold it off to the side, since Pockets is in the way. Planets and stars rise up off the page as usual, but this time a glowing red line snakes its way from our current location through two wormholes and across three more galaxies. "He wants us to go in the complete opposite direction of Libra 6!" I tell them.

"Can't be helped," Pockets says, switching off his screen. "We've got a princess to rescue."

Chapter Three:
A Dark Landing

Akbar's Floating Rest Stop is only a little bit out of our way, so that's where we head to drop Bloppy off. I'm excited to see the place again. Since it's full of aliens from all over, Bloppy won't have to worry about standing out.

"You'll only be here for a few hours, tops," Dad promises Bloppy as we enter Akbar's enormous gift shop. "I left two messages at headquarters, and they'll send another space taxi to take you the rest of the way. Okay?"

Bloppy's eyes are big and round. He is actually taking the news pretty well. Personally, I think he's relieved that he's not getting to his new job so quickly.

"Do you still need this?" I ask Bloppy, pointing to his name tag.

He nods. "We all wear them where I'm from. This way we can greet everyone by name."

"I like that idea," I say, reaching over to straighten it for him. Then we all shake his hand, even Pockets. Dad presses some money into Bloppy's palm. "Go have a skate at the new rink," Dad says, pointing to a sign advertising a new roller rink at Akbar's. "Or browse the bookshop. There's always a great selection of books from across the universe."

I know Dad feels terrible about making Bloppy wait for another driver. But our jobs as ISF deputies have to come first. We wave as we back out of the gift shop. Goop splatters on the floor as Bloppy waves back. I'm sorry to leave him, too.

"This is a tricky mission," Pockets says once we're on our way. "As your map shows, we'll be going to planet Tri-Dark. This planet—like Earth—is not aware of alien life in the universe. It is like life in medieval times, with castles and knights and horse-drawn carts. We'll have to hide our modern technology and disguise ourselves."

"Awesome!" I shout. "Can I be a knight? I've always wanted to wear armor and swing a sword."

He shakes his head. "You'll need more than costumes to blend in. I will alter your molecular structure with my Atomic Assembler."

"I only understood two words in that sentence," I tell him.

"I will make you look different," Pockets says plainly.

"What about you?" Dad asks him.

"They have cats on Tri-Dark, so I have no need to change."

"So you still get to be you," Dad says, "while Archie and I get turned into aliens?"

"Pretty much," Pockets admits. "But I will have to pretend to be a normal house pet again, so it won't be all fun and games for me, either."

"I'll promise not to scratch you behind the ears, if that helps," Dad says, grinning. "So, what's the mission?"

"King Argon owns a long walking stick—it's like a cane—that he calls the Staff of Power," Pockets begins. "He claims that it has magical powers and that it once destroyed a forest. I don't think it's true. Magic is only science that's not yet understood."

"So says the talking cat!" I comment.

Pockets pretends to ignore me and continues. "Anyway, B.U.R.P. must believe the staff has some kind of power—they took the king's only daughter, Princess Viola, and sent a ransom note insisting he hand over the staff in exchange for her safe return. We will have to find her before he gives the staff to B.U.R.P. Our undercover ISF agent was able to send the princess's last known location before his signal disappeared."

I quickly look at the map again. "A few more minutes until we cross into Tri-Dark's atmosphere. If the people there don't know about aliens and spaceships, what will happen when they see our taxi land?"

"They have not invented electric lights yet," Pockets replies. "So the planet will be totally dark at night. Can you fly this thing without the headlights?"

"Fly, yes," Dad says. "Land? No. I guess I should say I've never had to find out."

"No time like the present, then," Pockets says. "How long till we enter the atmosphere, Archie?"

"About three minutes."

"Not much time," he says. "Use your map to find a safe spot to land where our approach might be hidden."

I tap the image of the planet floating above my right knee. It gets larger. I stretch it out until I can see details like buildings and rivers. "Here!" I point to a wooded area with a clearing in the middle. "It's behind a large hill and looks far away from everything else."

"Good," Pockets says. "That hill should block us in case anyone is looking up. Now turn off the lights."

Dad and I exchange a quick glance, and

then we are in total darkness. The can't-even-see-my-hand-in-front-of-my-face kind of darkness. "Um, how am I supposed to guide us down to the surface if I can't see the map?"

"Night vision goggles!" Pockets declares, handing a pair to each of us.

"Why didn't you tell us earlier that you had these?" Dad asks.

"I can't be expected to remember *everything* in these pockets!" he replies.

We quickly put them on. The dark outline of the planet rises up right in front of us! Dad tilts the wings and lowers the wheels to slow us down, but we're coming in fast. My first reaction is to shut my eyes tight from fear, but I'm pretty sure that won't help me guide the taxi. I force myself to check the map. "We're only about three hundred feet away, Dad."

I point out the window and shout, "There's the clearing!" A few seconds later, the wheels touch ground. Instead of gliding along smoothly, though, the taxi bumps up and down. It sounds like rocks are hitting the underside of the car.

When we roll to a stop, Dad shuts off the engines. No one moves.

Then Pockets asks, "Does anybody else smell popcorn?"

Chapter Four:
Is There Something Different About Me?

Apparently, if you drive over a cornfield, the heat from your car will pop some of the kernels. Woo-hoo! I open the door and take a deep breath. Nothing better than freshly popped popcorn! "Can we eat some?" I ask Dad as we all climb out. "It smells *soooo* good!"

"Not a chance," Dad says. "What would your mother say if I let either of you eat something that I drove over with the car?"

Pockets and I share a disappointed look, but I guess I can see his point.

"That's the way into town," Pockets says, pointing to a road leading away from the clearing. The goggles make everything look shades of red, but I can see almost as well as in daytime. He checks his screen. "The princess was last seen about a mile away. That's where we'll start searching in the morning. For now let's move the car as close to the woods as possible."

"Will do," Dad says, climbing back in. A few seconds later the car makes a whirring sound, followed by a chugging sound.

He tries again. Now a high-pitched whine fills the air. It sounds even squeakier than Minerva the mouse from headquarters.

Dad climbs back out. "Something must have gotten damaged when we landed," he says. He lies down on his back and slides under the car. A few minutes later he comes out, wiping grease and dirt off his face.

"I can repair it," he says, "but it will take a day or two." He turns to me. "I'll need to stay with the taxi, Archie. Do you want to go on the mission with Pockets? I know he will protect you. Or you're welcome to stay with me."

I can tell it's not easy for Dad to give me the choice to go without him. And honestly, my first reaction is to wrap myself around his leg and tell him I'll stay. But Pockets can't talk to anyone on this planet. He'll need me along to help. Plus, I want to see the knights in shining armor and the moats and the castles, and I'd miss all that if I stayed here.

"I'll go on the mission, Dad," I tell him, hoping I sound braver than I feel.

"That's the spirit, Archie!" Pockets says, slapping me on the back. "Now, let's get this car hidden before our cover is blown."

Even with Pockets's mega-strength, it takes a lot of huffing and puffing to roll the taxi across the field to the woods. When we finally get there, Pockets pulls out a skinny metal can. He shakes it and aims the nozzle into the air. A light mist sprays out and coats the entire car. Before

I can blink, the car shimmers brightly, then disappears!

"Where'd the taxi go?" I ask, eyes wide behind my goggles.

"It's still here," Pockets says. "You can touch it."

"Really?" I reach out my hand and slowly lean in. Sure enough, my hand touches the still-warm hood. "Wow! What is that stuff?"

"It's called Camo-It-Now." He tucks the can away. "It makes whatever you spray blend into the background."

I run my hand over the invisible car. This is so cool! I could do this all night!

"Come," Pockets says, as though reading my mind. "I suggest we all get some sleep. I'll wake you at dawn."

In less than a minute, Pockets has set up two inflatable mattresses with sleeping bags on them. He waits until I take off my goggles and climb into one of them, and then he curls up at the bottom.

"You are one handy cat to have around," Dad says, fluffing his pillow. But Pockets is already purring in his sleep and doesn't hear.

Dad's own snores soon join in. I stare into the night sky. Without any lights or pollution, the stars in this galaxy are so bright. I can't see the constellations I know from home. No Big Dipper or Orion's Belt. That's the last thought I have before Pockets jumps on my chest and says, "Rise and shine, young Morningstar!"

"Oomph!" I push him off. "Really, Pockets? Don't you know how much you weigh?"

Pockets jumps on Dad next. "Five more minutes," he mumbles.

"No can do!" Pockets says, sounding way too cheery for this early hour. I sit up, still groggy. The sun is just beginning to rise. It looks a lot like Earth's sun, maybe a little bigger.

"We've got to turn you into aliens," Pockets says, "then find the princess and keep the king from handing over the Staff of Power. All before breakfast!"

Dad and I climb out of our sleeping bags and stretch.

Pockets fiddles with something that looks like a television remote, but I'm pretty sure it's not. "Now stand still," he says. "This won't hurt a bit."

Before I even finish yawning, a buzzing runs through my body, followed by a not-so-gentle tugging. It's as though my arms and legs are being pulled in different directions. I try to talk, but my mouth won't move. I look to Dad for help, but Dad doesn't look like Dad anymore! I mean, I can still tell it's him, but instead of his brown hair and the goatee on his chin, he is bald with a bushy green beard. He also has three large eyes, all in a row. And is that...? Yup! A third arm has sprouted below his left one.

And did I mention he's wearing a dress?

"Archie! Is that you?" Dad blinks.

"It's me, Dad!" I wave my arms. Thankfully I have only two, but they seem longer than they used to. When I rest them at my sides, they reach my knees!

"Why don't I have three arms, too?" I ask.

"People here don't grow them until they're adults," Pockets explains.

Dad reaches for his face with his extra arm. He gives a little gasp when he finds the third eye between his other two. I suddenly realize I can see things to my left and right that I should only be able to see by turning my head! "Do I have three eyes, too?" I ask him.

"You sure do," Dad says. "And long orange hair." I can tell he's trying not to laugh. "Maybe you should braid it to keep it off your face," he suggests.

I swing my head from side to side. My hair reaches past my shoulders! I like to keep my hair on the longer side, but this is crazy!

"That must be how boys wear it here," Pockets says. "The Atom Assembler is programmed to keep up with the local customs."

Dad looks down at his legs. "Is that why I'm wearing this dress?"

Pockets chuckles, then shakes his head. "That's awkward. Let me fix my error."

He adjusts a knob on the assembler. Dad's legs jerk a bit, and suddenly he's wearing long brown pants, like the ones I have on.

Dad looks down, relieved. Then his hand flies up to his head. He finally realizes his hair is gone. Dad is very proud of his hair. "It'll grow back, right?" he asks Pockets in a panicky voice.

"You will return to normal at the end of our mission," Pockets promises, tucking the assembler into a pocket. "Now we really must be on our way."

Dad pulls me aside. "Listen to what Pockets tells you," he says. "And don't go off on your own. We don't know the rules here."

"Okay." This will be the first time I've been on an alien world without Dad for longer than a few minutes. He gives me a three-armed hug, which feels weird but not altogether bad.

Chapter Five:
That Is the Biggest Cat
I Have Ever Seen

We head down the road toward the village. "Remember," Pockets says, "when we get to town I'll have to pretend to be your pet. I will stay close and whisper instructions. Don't talk to anyone or attract too much attention."

"I won't," I promise.

By the time we get into town, the main square is filling with men and women setting up booths to sell food and clothes. If it weren't for all the extra eyes and arms, I'd feel as if I'd stepped back in time on Earth.

Pockets is winding in and out of my legs like a regular cat. He whispers, "The last signal we got from our undercover officer came from a farmhouse on the other side of the town square. That will be our first stop."

I nod as we begin to cross the square. No one gives us a second glance. My disguise must be working!

Two boys—both with three eyes and long hair the same green as Dad's beard—run out of a house across the lane. They begin tossing a ball between them. One misses and the ball rolls right to my feet. I pick it up. It's made of wood, and very rough. The boys run over, and I hold it out to them. It makes me miss playing baseball with my friends at home. I haven't seen them very much lately.

"That is the biggest cat I have ever seen!" the older boy says, ignoring the ball. "Much bigger than the ones at the haunted castle by the river."

Haunted castle? That doesn't sound like a fun place to hang out.

The boy bends down beside Pockets. "Might my brother and I pet him?" he asks.

"Um, okay," I say. So much for not talking to anyone!

Pockets growls, and the boy stops, his hand outstretched.

"Pockets!" I say, like I'm scolding a real pet. "Not nice."

Pockets glares up at me before lowering his head so the kids can pet him.

"So soft!" the younger boy says, stroking Pockets on the head. The older one starts scratching Pockets under the neck. After a few seconds Pockets actually starts purring!

"Why does he have a circle of green around his tail?" the younger brother asks.

"Um..." I say, trailing off. I can't tell them the truth—that laser beams shoot out of it!

"Would you like to join our game?" the older one asks.

"Really? Thanks!"

Pockets stops purring and nudges me hard in the leg. The boys start explaining the rules. Pockets is working himself into a frenzy, turning in circles and pawing at the ground.

The boys look at him, concerned. "I think something is wrong with your cat," the younger one says. "That happened to ours right before he coughed up half a mouse."

Pockets makes a coughing-choking sound, and the boys scamper backward.

"Guess I'd better go take care of him," I tell them. "Nice meeting you!"

Pockets takes off across the square, and I run after him. He doesn't slow down until we reach a big red farmhouse on the outskirts of town, right where he said the ISF guard had disappeared.

I sit down and rest against the wall of a wooden storage shed.

"We must hurry to find the undercover guard," Pockets says, looking back down at his tracking device. "Where did he go after leaving this spot?"

"I don't think he went anywhere. Come listen." I wave him over to the shed, and we press our ears against the side.

"Snoring!" Pockets exclaims. He steps back and crouches low to the ground. Then he springs into the air, arches his back, and lands on the ledge of a small window. He swishes his tail around until it's in front of him, unhinges the tip, and uses the laser beam to melt a large hole in the glass. With a satisfied glance, he squeezes in.

I, however, use the door that is about

a foot away from the window. And not locked. When I step inside, he says, "Well sure, anyone could get in *that* way."

The small shed holds only three things— a bale of hay, a broken wheelbarrow, and the sleeping ISF officer with his back against the far wall.

"He's a cat!" I say in surprise. He looks like a bigger, grizzlier Pockets. He's definitely seen some action.

"Why are you surprised?" Pockets asks.

"You said there are ISF branches in every galaxy, so I figured he would be a different kind of alien."

"That makes sense," Pockets says. "But the best of the best are from Friskopolus." He says this last part with obvious pride. He bends down beside the giant cat. "This is Hector. He was in training with my dad. Good officer. A little grumpy."

"But if he was undercover as an alien, why is he back in his cat form?" I ask.

Pockets looks around and points to a yellow-tipped dart lying next to Hector. "Aha! Sleep serum! It reversed the Atom Assembler's changes. Perhaps he left us a clue before the serum took hold."

He whips out two of his huge magnifying glasses and says, "Look for anything unusual."

"Like this?" I ask, holding my magnifying glass over a patch of dust next to Hector's left paw. Spelled out in the dirt are the words GHOST CASTLE.

"That must be the same place the boys were talking about!"

"What better place to hide than where everyone is afraid to go?" Pockets says. "Excellent work, ISF deputy Morningstar!"

"Aw, I just got lucky," I say. "I saw his paw was stretched out, so I followed it, and there were the letters."

"That's not luck," Pockets says. "You recognized a clue, and it led to a bigger clue. That's what a good detective does." He pulls out a blanket and lays it over Hector. Then he tucks a small green teddy bear under the giant cat's arm. "That'll give him a chuckle when he wakes up," Pockets says before hurrying out the door.

CHAPTER SIX:
I Didn't Know Princesses Did That!

The river is about three miles away, and after mile two I'm hungry and, honestly, a little cranky. I'm tired of pushing the long hair away from my face, where it's started to stick from sweat. I've already snapped at Pockets twice just for pointing out the local plants and flowers. Finally he says, "Here, take this," and pulls out a paper bag. It's my snack from Mom! I thought I'd left it in the car.

"You're the best, Pockets." I hungrily chow down on Mom's famous peanut butter pancakes and slurp the hot chocolate. Much better! We finally reach the castle grounds and are greeted with painted wooden signs.

STAY AWAY.
TURN AROUND NOW.
DON'T EVEN THINK OF GETTING ANY CLOSER.

The castle walls are a tall, thick gray stone covered in green moss and ivy. The surrounding garden is full of dead plants and withered vines. It is not a welcoming place.

Pockets motions for me to join him behind a large tree. From here we can spy on the castle without being seen. Spying is actually a lot less exciting than I thought it would be. Basically, we stare at the old building and wait. I whisper to Pockets, "What's the point of having three eyes if they don't do anything cool like see through walls?"

"Good idea," he replies. He pulls out a pair of X-ray glasses and peeks around the side of the tree. If you've never seen a cat wearing X-ray glasses, it is truly something to behold.

"These aren't working," he says, stashing the glasses away. "That can only mean the

X-rays are being blocked. No one from Tri-Dark would be able to do that. B.U.R.P. must be inside."

I gulp. Something black darts past us, so close it stirs a little breeze on my legs. "What was that?" I ask, jumping to my feet.

Suddenly, more shapes come out of the woods. We are surrounded! But not by ghosts or knights or evil B.U.R.P. members.

We are surrounded by cats! Regular, normal-size cats who don't talk and don't carry a carload of stuff inside their fur.

They stream past us toward the castle. Pockets and I exchange a look, then run after them, careful to stay hidden by the trees. We find the cats pacing and meowing in front of a large wooden door.

"Someone must be feeding them," Pockets whispers.

Cat-loving criminals? That's a new one.

Sure enough, a minute later the door creaks open, scraping against the stone floor. An arm shoots out, leaves a bowl of milk, and shoots back inside. It reappears and adds another bowl, this one filled with brown lumps of meat. The cats crowd around, eagerly eating and drinking. The door opens a little further, and a small figure dressed in a black cape steps half-way out and looks around. Pockets and I scoot behind the tree again.

"Good kitties," a boy's voice says softly. "Aren't you such good kitties? Yes you are, yes you are!"

We risk another look. A hood covers

most of the boy's face, but from what I can tell, he doesn't seem to have long bright-colored hair. I can't see if he has three eyes or not. He takes turns to pet each of the cats, even the ones that have scraggly, tangled fur.

"This is our chance," Pockets whispers. "I'll blend in with the cats, then slip inside while the door's still open. When it is safe, I will unlock the door and let you in."

I look from Pockets to the group of cats and back again. "You don't look anything like those cats. You may not realize this, but you look—how should I put this?—very well fed."

He sucks in his cheeks. "How 'bout now?"

I laugh. "Nope. You're still huge."

"Maybe he won't notice," Pockets says. He lowers himself as far as he can get to the ground without lying down, then slinks toward the castle. Now he looks like a cat pretending to be a snake. Yeah, I'm pretty sure the kid's gonna notice him.

The cloaked boy's back is turned, and for a few seconds Pockets actually does manage to mingle. A few cats sniff the new arrival, but most are too busy eating to notice. A little black cat catches sight of Pockets and starts meowing. Pockets tries to gently bat his admirer away, but he keeps coming back, rubbing up against Pockets's legs and looking up adoringly. The boy turns to see what is causing the commotion.

"And who are you?" he asks, bending to

scratch Pockets on his head. "I haven't seen you around here, and you are not easy to miss! You're very soft. Are you someone's lost pet?"

Pockets meows in response, then squeezes between the boy's legs and pretends to head toward the bowl of milk. The boy turns away, and Pockets darts through the door. The little black cat trots right in after him. A moment later the dishes are empty and the boy returns inside. The cats slowly scatter.

I run from behind my tree and try the door.

Locked.

I lean against the rough stone wall and push the hair away from my face for the hundredth time. Maybe I *should* have let

Dad braid it! Who knows how long it will take Pockets to get me in? Maybe this is one of his tests where he makes me see if I can figure it out by myself. If it is, I don't want to fail. I look around again. I really am alone here.

There's a window about twenty feet above me. I'm going to have to climb the walls by digging my fingers and toes into the little cracks between the stones. I bet my extra-long arms will help make it easier. I take a deep breath, pretend I'm a brave knight on a quest, and slip off my shoes before I can chicken out.

GASP!

I only have two toes! And they're really far apart, like one is where the big toe would go and one is where the pinkie would go. Only these both look like big toes. I flex them and they move, like they've always been there. *So weird!*

Before I have a chance to test how well they would grip the wall, something lands on my head. It's a rope!

I look up to find Pockets sticking his head out the window. He waves for me to take the rope. I'm slightly disappointed that I won't get to try scaling the wall, but only slightly.

I quickly slip my shoes back on and begin to climb the rough rope. I tell myself this is not at all like the time in gym class when I tried to climb the rope and my shorts fell down in front of the whole class. "Nope," I say out loud, "not like that at all." I soon reach the top and am proud to say that my pants are still safely around my waist.

The room is cramped and dark. The walls are covered with paintings and tapestries showing scenes of knights having jousts.

"Seen any ghosts yet?" I ask, landing on the carpeted floor with both feet.

Pockets shakes his head. "But I did find the princess. She's being kept in a room upstairs."

"And you made a friend!" I say, pointing to the little black cat who had followed Pockets into the castle.

"Very funny," Pockets says. "He won't leave me alone."

I bend down to pet the cat, but he pulls back and rubs up against Pockets instead.

"Now listen," Pockets says. "We have to find a way to get to Princess Viola. There are two B.U.R.P. guards standing outside her room. We should—"

But before he can finish talking, the door creaks open and my heart starts thudding. Pockets pushes me into a dark corner of the room. I hold my breath.

"There you are, big kitty!" the boy's voice says. To my horror, he swoops Pockets into his arms, groaning a little at the cat's weight, and carries him out of the room! The door swings shut behind them, but not before I hear the boy say, "We're going to play together all day!"

For a minute I don't move. The little black cat is pawing at the closed door, meowing. Do I go after them? What would

Pockets want me to do? I replay the scene in my mind. Pockets could have defended himself. He could have used any of the gadgets in his pockets, or even his own strength to fight off the boy, but he didn't. He just pretended to be a regular cat. That must mean he had something to gain by being taken. The only thing I can think of is that by going along, he'll be able to find out what B.U.R.P. plans to do with the Staff of Power once they get it.

That means that it's up to *me* to rescue the princess!

I think for a minute, looking around the small room. I don't see any way out besides the window and the door. I wish I'd thought to bring my space map. It worked when we were flying underwater on the planet

Nautilus; maybe it would have shown me how to get to the princess.

It's doubly hard to think because the little black cat is running in circles around the room and it's making me dizzy. He finally darts over to one wall and starts pawing at a tapestry hanging there. If he keeps pulling on it, he's going to rip the fabric. He finally nudges it aside and ducks behind it. I look closer. Where'd he go?

I pull the tapestry back, and instead of seeing the wall behind it, I spot an open doorway! Pockets's new friend found a secret passageway! He must have felt a breeze. I'll have to remember that for the next time I find myself locked in a maybe-haunted castle. I pause for only one more second, then run straight through, letting the tapestry fall into place behind me.

This turns out to be a mistake. It's completely dark in here. If only I'd thought to bring those night vision goggles!

After a minute my eyes begin to adjust. I blink. Yes! I can see the outline of the damp stone walls and the uneven steps in front of me. I rub my eyes, and things get even clearer. These new eyes may not be able to see through walls, but they can see in the dark!

I scramble up the stairs, not knowing where I'm headed, just that I have to go up. The stairwell twists and turns. I find the black cat curled up on a stair, cleaning his ears with his paw. He doesn't even glance up as I step past him.

I stop when I hear a faint noise coming from the other side of the wall. It sounds like...burping? Do ghosts burp?

There it is again, followed by a brief giggle.

"Ack!" I jump back as something soft rubs against my leg. It takes a second to realize it's only that cat again! But now I can't keep my balance, and I go headfirst into the wall beside me.

Only it *isn't* a wall! It's a door painted to *look* like a wall! The door swings open, and I go crashing right through it.

I land hard on the stone floor of a brightly lit room. A yellow-haired, three-eyed girl stands above me with her hands on her hips. She glares at me, burps, and says, "Ever heard of knocking?"

Then she burps again.

This princess is *nothing* like the ones in the fairy tales!

Chapter Seven:
The Great Escape

I quickly jump to my feet. "Sorry to burst in," I say, rubbing my sore butt. Then I stop, because that looks weird. "But hey, I found you!"

She looks me up and down as the little black cat winds in and out of her legs. Her face softens. "Yes, you found me. But who ARE you? I've never seen you before. You're not with *them*, are you?" On the word *them*, she crumples her nose like she smells something bad.

"No, no, I'm here to rescue you," I promise her.

She glances down at her boots. "And this is your cat?"

I shake my head. "I'm actually here with a different cat. He has bottomless pockets."

"Huh?" she asks.

Why did I say that? "Never mind," I add quickly. "Let's just get out of here before they find us."

"Sorry about the burping before," she says, grabbing her cloak from the back of a chair. "You wouldn't believe the gassy stuff they've been feeding me! Beans and broccoli for every meal!"

"It's all right," I say. "I have a three-year-old sister. You wouldn't believe the things that come out of her."

She smiles and says, "I can't believe I didn't think to check for any secret doors in the walls. I feel foolish."

"Don't feel bad. B.U.R.P. is very tricky."

"We're still talking about my burping?" she says. "I said I was sorry. I know it's not very princess-like."

"No, no, this is a different kind of burp. It's the name of the group who took you."

The princess's brows squish together in confusion. "No one *took* me. I was invited here by circus performers," she says. "They were dressed up in colorful costumes and masks, and they invited me to come see a play they were performing at the haunted castle." She pauses, then grumbles, "Never did see any play."

I tilt my head toward her. "Didn't your parents ever tell you not to go wandering off with strangers?"

"Yes, smarty-pants. But my bodyguard said it was okay."

I think of Hector asleep in that shed. Somehow I don't picture him letting her go off with anyone. "Did he really?"

She looks down. "Well, no. But he wasn't around for some reason and I wanted an adventure. I admit, it didn't turn out so well. Why would they keep me here?"

"Basically, they're after the Staff of Power," I tell her. "But we really need to leave now."

Her eyes widen. "What would a group of circus performers want with the Staff of Power?"

I roll my eyes. This girl is *not* getting it. "They aren't circus performers," I explain as patiently as possible. "B.U.R.P. is a criminal organization trying to take over the universe."

"What's a universe?"

Oops! I can't explain what the universe is without telling her about all the other planets and galaxies, and I'm sure that Pockets would forbid that. So I just shake my head and say, "I'll explain later. We have to go."

She nods and runs down the stairs ahead of me. Her heavy boots clatter loudly on the stairs, and I want to suggest maybe she take them off, but I'm not going to tell a princess what to do.

We haven't gotten very far when we hear, "Stop right there!" We double our speed. I have no idea where the stairs actually lead. Hopefully not to a solid stone wall. Or a dungeon!

Suddenly, laser beams go shooting over our heads! The princess blinks in shock and stumbles on the stairs. "What is that? I've never seen a light so bright."

I reach out to steady her. "Um, maybe the sun is shining in through cracks in the walls?" I hold my breath, hoping she buys that story.

"I guess," she says uncertainly.

"The staff is ours," a man's voice shouts. "There's no escape!"

"I recognize that voice," the princess says. "He's one of the circus performers!"

This time I don't bother to correct her. Especially since the man might be right! I don't see any escape.

"Oh yes there is!" another voice shouts from below. *This* voice I know! Pockets bursts into view, waving us forward. As soon as we pass by him on the stairs, he pulls out a gadget I've seen him use once before—the invisible force field! He aims it at the stairs above us. One after the other, the two men who were chasing us run right into it! They bounce backward and wind up tangled together, shouting and waving their arms and legs. The princess looks at Pockets, and then at the men who *don't* have three eyes who just ran into something she can't see. Then she crumples gracefully to the floor.

"Quick," Pockets shouts. "Grab her and follow me."

"But she's as big as me," I say, bending down. "What if I drop her?"

"You're stronger than you look," he says.

He's right! My arms aren't only long, they're really strong! I easily lift the princess and carry her over my shoulder. The B.U.R.P. guys are still trapped behind the force field, but it won't take long till they figure out a way around it.

I hurry after Pockets, who has found a

back door. Once outside he heads right for the stables and unties a huge white horse from a post. A rickety-looking wooden cart is attached to the horse with a frayed rope.

Pockets points to the cart. "Are you okay riding back there with the princess?"

I'm really not. It looks like a carnival ride my mother would never let me go on. "Do I have a choice?" I ask.

"Certainly," he says, slipping his paws in the spurs. "You can always stay here with B.U.R.P., the ghosts, and a lot of hungry cats."

Suddenly, the cart doesn't look so bad. Holding the princess, I climb in. It sags and groans under our weight.

The horse starts to move. We don't even get off the castle grounds before the

back door bangs open. "Hurry," I shout to Pockets. "They got around the force field!"

The princess stirs. Her eyes flutter open. She takes in the scene around her, and then her eyes bulge. "Is that a giant cat riding horseback?" she asks.

I nod.

"And the men with the strange lights are chasing us?" she asks, looking out the back of the cart as it bounces down the dirt road.

"Yes," I say. "And there's a boy our age here, too, somewhere."

The men are getting closer. I can see their faces clearly now. They look close to human, but with longer noses and shorter legs.

"But...but what happened to them?"

she asks with a shaky voice. "Where's their middle eye? And why do they only have two arms?"

I try to think fast. "Um, maybe they come from far away where people look different? You know, like from the other side of the river."

She shakes her head. "I've been to the other side of the river. My bodyguard, Hector, takes me there sometimes for jousting lessons. Girls aren't supposed to joust, but Hector's the best. So I know they don't have two-armed, two-eyed men and cats who ride horseback there."

The men start firing their lasers again. One beam burns a hole in the side of the cart! The princess and I scramble away from the flames. Pockets whirls around and with one paw shoots a stream of foam to put out the fire.

The princess begins breathing heavily, her eyes wild with surprise. The men can't keep up with our horse and finally fall behind.

"I'm going to take a shortcut to the castle," Pockets shouts to us. "It'll be a bumpy ride, but we must get there before B.U.R.P. does, and we don't want to be seen!"

The princess turns to ask me, "Did that cat just talk to us? I thought I heard him speak on the stairs, but I figured I imagined it."

I nod, since obviously I can't deny it. "Yeah, he can do that. I know, it's weird."

"Really weird," she agrees.

"His name is Pockets," I tell her.

She smiles. "Let me guess—he's the cat with the bottomless pockets?"

I know she's teasing me, but I don't mind. "Yup," I say.

"So I know your cat's name, but I don't know *your* name," she says. "Are you training with my father to be a knight?"

I laugh. "No. I mean, I wish I were. I'm just a regular kid. My name is Archie Morningstar."

Pockets suddenly cuts to the left, across the nearest farm. He wasn't kidding about it being bumpy. The princess and I bounce nearly three feet in the air.

"Sorry about that," Pockets shouts back at us.

"Well," the princess says, gripping the

sides of the cart tightly, "I did want an adventure!"

I can't believe it, but we make it to the princess's castle without losing a wheel or throwing up or being attacked by B.U.R.P. again. The king and a dozen knights in armor come streaming out of the front gate. This castle is about *ten times* the size of the haunted castle. It's the biggest building I've ever seen up close.

The king is wearing a tall gold crown and a red cape. The Staff of Power must be the thin metal pole he is waving above his head. I expected it to be covered in gold and jewels, but it doesn't look much different from the rod that holds up the curtains in our living room.

Before she jumps out of the cart,

Princess Viola leans over and whispers, "I'm pretty sure you're not just a regular kid, Archie Morningstar. Thank you for rescuing me." And then she kisses me on the cheek!

My hand flies up to my face, and I'm sure that my cheeks must be bright red. Pockets chuckles from atop his horse.

The princess runs up to her father and they hug. Then the king turns to us. "I demand to know what is going on. First my daughter stays out all night, worrying me to no end, and now what looks like a giant cat returns her on my missing guard's horse."

"The cat can talk!" the princess tells her father. "I've heard him!"

"Meow?" Pockets says meekly.

The princess puts her hands on her hips and glares at Pockets. "Very funny. I heard you before."

"She's telling the truth," a deep voice says from behind us. I whirl around to find Hector, the ISF bodyguard. And he's holding up the two B.U.R.P. guys by their shirt collars, one in each paw. The boy in the black cape must have escaped. "Are you all right, Princess Viola?" Hector asks.

The knights draw their swords and form a protective circle around the king and the princess. The princess stares at the huge cat from inside the circle of knights. "Hector?" she asks. "Is that you? It sounds like you, but how can it be that you are a cat now, when before you were a man?"

"It is still me, Your Highness," Hector says, bowing slightly. "I am sorry to have hidden my true identity from you, but it was for the betterment of your world. I am an Intergalactic Security Force officer. I was sent here to protect you and the Staff of Power." He tilts his head at Pockets. "The talking cat you mentioned is a fellow ISF officer. He was sent here to help."

In one swift move, Pockets leaps off the horse and onto the back of one of the bad guys. A second later, the guy is in handcuffs. Hector does the same with the other guy.

The king looks from one cat to the other. "Who sent you two? In what land can cats speak and catch criminals? And why are these men so strange-looking? They only have two eyes and two hands!" He shudders.

I'm pretty sure the king won't buy my explanation about the other side of the river, so I keep my mouth shut.

"Just give us the staff and we will be on our way," one of the men demands.

"The staff?" the king repeats.

"Didn't you get their note demanding the Staff of Power in exchange for Princess Viola?" Pockets asks, speaking in front of the king for the first time.

"What note?" the king asks.

"This one," Hector says. He reaches into a pocket of fur and pulls out a scroll. He hands the scroll to the king.

"Hector's got pockets in his fur, too!" I whisper to Pockets.

"It's a space cat thing," he whispers back.

"I was able to grab this out of the messenger's bag before it reached the castle," Hector explains. "I couldn't risk your handing over the staff."

The king reads B.U.R.P.'s demands. "I will take it from here," he tells Pockets and Hector. To his knights he says, "Do not let these criminals escape." The knights step forward and place heavy armored hands on the bad guys' shoulders.

Pockets pulls out his phone. "I have to call my father," he explains.

Seems like a strange time to say hi, but when his father answers, Pockets goes into this whole story about how we tried to fit in here, but in the end we had no choice and now the king knows too much. His father's voice booms through the other end of the phone. "You know what you have to do, Pilarbing Fangorious!"

Pockets tries to argue. "Not that! Please, Dad, anyone but—"

His dad hangs up. Pockets grits his teeth, then makes another call. This time I don't hear anything from the other end. But a moment later, a shimmer appears in the air. Before I can blink, a tiny red alien with waving antennae and one big eye stands in front of us. His little round spaceship hovers a few feet above the ground. I gasp in surprise, and I'm not the only one. One of the knights actually *faints*! The king pulls the princess close, but she squirms away to get a closer look.

If Pockets is trying to keep them from knowing about life on other planets, he's not doing a very good job of it by bringing this guy here.

"Hey!" I say to the new arrival. "Where have I seen you before?"

The alien totally ignores me and hurries up to Pockets. He bows deeply. "You called for me, oh noble, glorious one! I always knew this day would come. How can I be of help?"

And I thought Bloppy and that little black cat were fans of Pockets. They've got nothing on this guy! I admit, I'm a little jealous. He's supposed to be MY cool cat!

Pockets grimaces. "Hello, Feemus," he forces himself to say through clenched teeth. "Do what you do best."

The alien salutes Pockets like he's in the army. "Yes, sir!" he says. He turns his one-eyed gaze onto the crowd. Then a beam of red light shoots between his two antennae, and everyone except him, me, the horse, Pockets, and Hector stands

frozen in the middle of whatever they were doing.

Even a bird has stopped in midflight! The princess has one arm out, reaching for Feemus, who steps politely away.

Pockets and Hector spring into action. Pockets slips the staff from the king's hand and replaces it with one almost exactly the same size and shape. "Curtain rod from the haunted castle," he explains with a wink. That cat thinks of everything.

Hector grabs the two bad guys and somehow squeezes them into Feemus's tiny spaceship. He then runs over to the frozen princess and pats her lovingly on the head. "I will miss you, little one," he tells her. "You've got pluck and a natural curiosity. It will serve you well. Once the

Staff of Power is gone from here, you shall be safe again." He pulls out a jousting helmet from one of his pockets and tucks it under Viola's arm. Then he grabs the stuffed bear Pockets had left with him in the shed and sticks it inside the helmet for her to find. With a final bow to the frozen king, he joins his prisoners in Feemus's spaceship.

"I don't understand," I say to Pockets, who is busy untying the horse from the cart. "How did the little red guy freeze everyone? What happens when they unfreeze and we're gone?"

"They won't remember us," Pockets explains. "Feemus has the ability to slow down time until it almost stops. He will replace their memories of the past day and then return them to their normal time frame."

I take one last look around. "Princess Viola won't remember me at all?"

"Sorry, but no," he says.

I hold my hand to my cheek. I will definitely remember her.

Feemus approaches Pockets. "Are you ready, oh amazing one, oh great leader?"

Pockets groans. "Please stop calling me things like that."

"But I am the head of your fan club," Feemus says. "How can I not be thrilled to be in your presence?"

"Fan club?" I repeat in disbelief. "You have a *fan club*?"

"I don't want to talk about it," Pockets says. He turns around and hops up onto the horse's back. He holds out his paw, I grab it, and he hoists me up behind him. I wrap my arms around his belly.

"Wait twenty minutes and then unfreeze them," Pockets instructs Feemus. "That will give us a chance to get back to our landing site and take off. Give the princess the memory that she wandered to the haunted castle and found some stray cats. Perhaps she will go back to feed them and will bring the gardens back to life. It may fulfill her need for adventure a bit."

Feemus bows again. "Yes, Your Wonderfulness. Thank you again for allowing me to be of service. You are truly the bravest, smartest, most—"

I don't hear what other compliments Feemus was about to give, because Pockets turns the horse around and begins to gallop toward the cornfield. I hold on tighter. They should make seat belts on these things!

A memory comes rushing back to me. I lean into Pockets. "Now I remember where I've seen that guy! You wouldn't let him sit with us for lunch at Akbar's a few weeks ago. Why wouldn't you?"

"He's always following me around," Pockets says as we reach the town square. "It was kind of flattering in the beginning, but now it's just embarrassing. He's so... *enthusiastic.*" We pass at least twenty people, all frozen in the midst of eating, talking, shopping, or walking. I look for the boys, but they aren't playing their game anymore.

"I think he's sweet," I tell him. "I hope we see him again."

"Trust me, we will."

"Dad!" I shout, scrambling off the horse the second we arrive back at the taxi. I was half-afraid he'd be frozen like everyone else, but he's not. He runs over and scoops me up while Pockets dissolves the camo-spray and makes the taxi reappear.

"Archie! How was it? Did you find the princess before the king gave B.U.R.P. the staff?"

"It turns out he didn't even know they were after it," I explain. "Hector the cat stopped the note before it got to the king, but I found the princess and she thought she was going to see a circus! And did you know Pockets has a fan club?"

"Hector the cat?" he asks. "A circus? A fan club? Sounds like you've got a long story to tell me."

"It will have to wait for the ride home," Pockets says. "We need to leave right now." He jumps into the backseat of the taxi and settles in for his usual post-adventure nap.

"Ahem," Dad says, clearing his throat. "Forget something?" He waves his third arm in the air.

"Oops," Pockets says. He pulls out the Atom Assembler and zaps us both. It tingles just as much as last time. I'm going to miss my three eyes. It was kinda cool being able to see in the dark without those goggles.

"Hey, Dad," I ask as we climb in the

front seat, "did you know we only had two toes on this planet?"

He is busy admiring his full head of hair in the rearview mirror and doesn't hear me. It will just have to be my little secret.

Chapter Eight:
Happily Ever After

Once we are safely out of sight of Tri-
Dark, we can finally relax. Pockets sends
a message to his dad. He reports that
the cat-loving boy in the black cloak is
an important member of B.U.R.P. and
that he is still on the loose. He makes

sure to mention my role in helping on the mission, which is very nice of him. Then he puts away his screen and pulls out his pillow.

Dad calls headquarters to check in. Minerva is finally back, but she is not happy.

"Morningstar!" she shouts. "I just got a call from the taxi depot on Libra 6. They said your pickup—one Mr. Bloppy—never arrived yesterday. Explain?"

"Didn't you get my messages?" Dad asks. "We had to drop Bloppy at Akbar's. I told you that we had an important mission and that I needed another driver to take him the rest of the way."

"I received no such message," Minerva says.

Dad and I exchange a worried look. "So he's still at Akbar's?" Dad asks.

"I have no idea," Minerva says.

"We're on our way," Dad says.

"I blame that cat," Minerva grumbles.

Dad switches off the com. I map out the fastest way to get there.

When we arrive, Dad, Pockets, and I run all over Akbar's calling Bloppy's name. We keep asking, but no one has seen him, which is strange because he's not someone you could easily miss. Plus, he's wearing a name tag. Pockets ducks into Barney's to grab us all some bagels (of course) while Dad and I keep looking. We wind up back where we started, in the gift shop. A sign on the wall catches my eye. It's different from the one we saw last time.

WHETHER YOU'VE GOT YOUR
OWN WHEELS OR NEED
TO BORROW OURS,
VISIT AKBAR'S ROLLER RINK!
WE NOW HAVE THE SHINIEST,
SMOOTHEST FLOORS THIS SIDE
OF THE VIRGO SUPERCLUSTER.
SO ROLL ON IN AND TAKE
A SPIN!

The shiniest, smoothest floors! I know someone who can make a floor supershiny!

Sure enough, we spot Bloppy as soon as we reach the roller rink. He's standing in the center of the rink, dripping goop everywhere. Creatures with all number of legs skate happily around him. He breaks into a huge grin when he sees us. He looks much happier than when we picked him up on Earth.

"Sal and Archie Morningstar!" he cries out. "How lovely to see you!"

We run onto the rink, slipping and sliding as we go. "We are so glad to see you, too," Dad says. "I'm sorry! There was a mix-up and no taxi was sent to get you yesterday. But I can drive you now."

Bloppy's smile doesn't fade. "Your dropping me here was the best thing that could have happened. This is the perfect job for me. Everyone at Akbar's is so nice." He leans close to us and lowers his voice. "And I met a special someone." He tilts his head toward the other side of the rink.

At first I think I'm seeing Bloppy in the mirror, but *this* Bloppy is pink instead of orange and is wearing a pink bow on her head. I can't read her name tag from this far away, but I can see she's wearing one.

Dad grins and slaps Bloppy on the shoulder. "Way to go, dude. She's a keeper."

"I know," Bloppy says, waving to the girl. She waves back with both arms. As she does, huge, gooey pink globs fall from her hands and splat across the floor. The skaters around her cheer.

We promise Bloppy we will visit whenever we're in the neighborhood. He hugs us both good-bye. I don't know what Pockets was making such a big fuss about. It's a nice, cozy, only mildly oozy hug.

It's dark again by the time we finally arrive home to our apartment on Earth.

Mom gives me a huge hug and says I look older, which I'm sure I don't, even if I did rescue a princess.

Penny's light is still on, so I go in to say good night. She looks up at me with big, sleepy eyes. "Story?" she asks.

Even though I'm *sooooo* tired, I sit down on the edge of her bed and begin. "Once upon a time, there was a beautiful princess named Viola who liked to joust. And when she ate beans, well, she could burp louder than anybody!"

Penny giggles.

"One day she met a group of circus performers and..."

Penny snores. She and Pockets and Dad have a lot in common—they all fall asleep quickly and make a lot of noise

when they sleep. The rest of the story will have to wait till tomorrow night. Unless I'm off on another adventure! For now, though, I'm happy to be back home. As I get up to leave, Pockets comes in, jumps onto the bed, turns in circles a few times, and then curls up and begins licking his paws.

"Hey, Pockets," I whisper. "Is that Feemus outside Penny's window?"

"Aaaaahhh!" He scrambles off the bed and zips underneath it.

I'll tell him I was only kidding in the morning.

THREE SCIENCE FACTS TO IMPRESS YOUR FRIENDS AND TEACHERS

1. **LIGHT** plays an important role in Archie's adventure to planet Tri-Dark, where electricity hasn't been invented yet. Light is made up of particles called **PHOTONS**, and they travel in waves, like the kind you'd see in the ocean. Each color of visible light has a different wavelength—purple has the shortest, and

red has the longest. Light will bounce off a mirror or bend in water.

2. Archie is not able to see many stars at home on Earth because of all the outside lights in the city at night. The light shines up into the sky, and then our atmosphere scatters it and sends it back down at us, blocking our view of the stars. Since there is no electric light on Tri-Dark, Archie is able to see all the stars clearly, as our ancestors would have been able to on Earth. LiGHt POLLUtioN not only blocks our ability to see into space, but it causes migrating birds to go off course, and it confuses nocturnal animals that come out at night and need the darkness. Light pollution also wastes energy by sending light into the sky, where it is not needed.

3. Archie's dad uses NiGHt ViSiON GOGGLES so he can see in the dark to land his space taxi on Tri-Dark. There are two types of night vision goggles. The first type is called iMaGE ENHaNCEMENt, which is the type Archie, his dad, and Pockets use in the story. The goggles collect any available light reflected off an object (even infrared, which the human eye normally can't see). The light is then passed through a series of lenses, allowing the person wearing the goggles to see in the dark. The other type of night vision goggles is called tHERMaL iMaGiNG. This type detects light that is emitted by objects in the form of heat, and allows the wearer to see the images based on how warm something is. This would be helpful if Archie was trying to find Pockets in the dark.

By Wendy Mass and Michael Brawer

Ⓛ Ⓑ

LITTLE, BROWN AND COMPANY
New York   Boston

To the amazing young readers of
Sparta, New Jersey:
Thank you all for coming along
for the ride.

CONTENTS

CHAPTER ONE:
Training Day

"Faster, Archie, faster!" Pockets shouts as I get closer. "Pretend a hippoctopus from Omega 9 is chasing you. He thinks you're dinner!"

Sneakers pounding on the sidewalk, I finally turn the corner and reach the courtyard behind our apartment building. I lean against the brick wall, panting. Pockets steps out from behind the large tree he was using as cover. Even though it's rare to find anyone back here besides me and my sister, Penny, it's best to be careful. No one can know that Pockets is actually a super intergalactic crime fighter and not just our giant, fluffy pet cat who sheds a lot and sleeps even more. He clicks his stopwatch and shakes his head in disapproval.

"What ... *pant pant* ... is a hippoctopus?" I ask. "Is that like a cross between a hippo ... *pant* ... and an octopus?"

Pockets's eyes dart left and right. When he's completely sure we're alone, he says, "Exactly. Only bigger, smellier, and with more arms. Now, let's go twice more around the building, this time backward."

I shake my head. "I need a break. I've been running for an hour straight while alternating between bouncing a tennis ball and jumping rope. I don't know if you've tried it, but it's pretty much impossible to do without looking totally ridiculous." In fact, my downstairs neighbor, Mr. Goldblatt, shouted *Oy vey!* when I ran/jumped/bounced by for the fifth time while he was walking his dog. He says that to me and my sister, Penny, a lot, usually while shaking his head in disbelief at the same time. He's cranky, but he's really nice, too. After I told him that Dad had taken me to Barney's Bagels and Schmear, Mr. Goldblatt was the one who explained that *schmear* can actually mean two things—the act of coating the bagel with a spread, such as cream cheese, or the cream cheese itself. Like THAT'S not confusing! I know he'd love to hear that aliens are real and that I've actually been on other planets, but Dad and I have to keep the space taxi thing—and especially our jobs as Intergalactic Security Force deputies—a secret.

"Part of your training is to improve your hand-eye coordination and balance," Pockets says. "As an ISF deputy, you have to be quick on your feet and ready to react in the blink of an eye." He tucks his stopwatch into one of the endlessly deep pockets hidden in his fur and then pulls out two pairs of sunglasses. He tosses me a pair and sticks the other on his face. For a cat, he can rock a pair of sunglasses like no one else I know.

"All right, you've earned a rest," he says. "You're actually pretty fast for a human boy."

I gratefully drop the rope and ball at my feet and take a long sip from my water bottle. "Are humans known for being slow?" I ask. "I mean, compared to people on other planets?"

"They are slower than approximately 9,356,110 other species."

"Wow, that's pretty slow."

Pockets shrugs. "Like everything, it's all in the way you look at it. You're also faster than at least sixteen billion species, if that makes you feel any better."

"It does, a little," I admit. "Let's hope I'm on one of *those* planets when something big and smelly with more than eight arms wants to eat me for dinner." I slip on my glasses. "So, what are these for? It's not very sunny out." The glasses make the courtyard look only a tiny bit darker.

"Slide your hand around the frame on the left until you feel a little switch," he instructs. "Then push it toward you."

I follow his instructions, and the lenses flicker. I blink in surprise. Instead of seeing Pockets next to the tree, which is what I'd been looking at, all I see is myself, standing in front of the wall. I turn my head from side to side, but the view doesn't change. It's like I'm frozen in place. That's weird! Then Pockets says, "I'm going to turn my head now," and suddenly I can see not only myself but also the sides of the building, the small laundry room window above my

head, and the jump rope in a heap on the ground. "I get it!" I say excitedly. "I'm seeing what *you're* seeing!"

"Correct. Now push the switch in the opposite direction and I will see what *you* see."

I push the switch. My view returns to normal. I walk in a circle around Pockets and ask, "Do you see yourself now?"

He grins and puts a paw on his hip. "I'm one handsome cat, aren't I? I don't believe I've ever seen my own rump before."

I giggle at the word *rump*. "Not sure you'll win any beauty contests, but you're all right as far as giant talking cats go." We both switch our glasses back to the regular setting.

Pockets reaches into his pocket and pulls out a wireless earpiece. I've seen him use one to talk long-distance with his dad, but I've never seen it up close. He holds out the tiny device and I grab it. "My own earpiece?" I ask, sticking it in my ear before he can change his mind. *"Oooohh!"*

It instantly molds to the shape of my ear-lobe and is so small I doubt anyone could see it unless they were peering into my ear from an inch away, which would be weird. "It tickles! Do I get to keep it?"

"For now," he says, sticking one in his own ear. "We will practice using them so we'll be able to communicate if we get separated on a mission. Hopefully, we won't have to worry about that, of course."

"Hey, I did okay on my own on our last mission, right? I rescued the princess by myself."

Pockets clears his throat. "Well, you may have had a *little* help."

Before I can argue, Mr. Goldblatt's tiny black pug, Luna, slowly trots into the courtyard, her leash trailing behind her.

Luna is old and half-blind, so I guess Mr. Goldblatt isn't worried about her running away before he catches up. She's still sharp enough to spot the yellow tennis ball at my feet, though, and pounces on it.

I bend down to pet her. "Hey there, Luna, old girl. How are you doing?" In response, she slobbers all over the ball. A little drool gets on my ankle and drips into my sock, but I don't mind.

"Don't make any sudden moves," a low, deep voice hisses in my ear.

CHAPTER TWO:
The Beast

I spin around but don't see anyone. And hey, where did Pockets go? The voice comes again. "What did I say about sudden moves! She's going to see me!"

"Who is this?" I say, straightening up. "Where are you?"

"It's *me*, obviously!" Pockets says in his normal voice.

I laugh and my hand goes up to my earpiece. I'd forgotten about it already! "It really feels like you're inside my head," I shout. "So you can hear me, too?"

"Of course I can hear you! Wouldn't be much of a communication device if it only went one way. And no need to shout."

"Okay, okay, I get it." I look behind the tree where he'd been hiding earlier, but I only find a squirrel picking apart an acorn. "Where are you?"

"Look up!"

The glasses help shade my eyes from the setting sun as I peer up into the branches. I spot Pockets's white tail swishing through the leaves about halfway up. "What are you doing up there?" I ask.

"Hiding from that beast," he replies.

I laugh. "Old Luna? She wouldn't hurt a fly. Or a cat, as the case may be." On hearing her name, Luna barks and rolls over, the ball tucked under one paw.

A few leaves flutter to the ground next to us. Then more leaves. Pockets is climbing higher.

"C'mon, Pockets, don't be scared," I tell him. "You're ten times the size of this dog. If you're really scared, you can put up a force field like you did when you didn't want to go to the groomer to get a haircut."

"Dogs are tricky," he insists. "It would get through somehow, I'm certain."

I start to tell him that Luna can barely

finish lunch without falling asleep, much less summon the strength to break through a force field, but he's not listening. "You should climb up here, too, Archie," he says. "Scaling trees is good practice. In fact, it's on our list for tomorrow."

I shake my head. "The last time I was in a tree, I met you! That turned out to be a pretty good tree. I'm sure this one would just be a disappointment after that one."

He starts to reply, but another, deeper, voice cuts into my earpiece. "Pilarbing? Can you hear me?"

"I can hear you, Father," Pockets says after settling himself directly on top of the tree. He looks like the world's largest Christmas tree ornament!

"Hi, Mr. Catapolitus!" I shout. "It's Archie."

"Young Morningstar?" the chief of the ISF asks. "What are you doing on this communication channel? And why are you shouting?"

Pockets replies for me. "We are testing out the earpieces, Father. I can switch to a private line if you prefer."

"No, this call concerns Archie, too."

"A new mission?" I ask. I start to jump up and down but catch myself. I *am* almost nine, after all.

"Maybe," he says. "But right now we have a mystery on our hands. We are tracking a very unusual break-in. The thieves are known agents of B.U.R.P. We cannot think of why the sneakiest criminal organization in the universe would take the risk, though. Pilarbing, you're the best officer we have when it comes to figuring out B.U.R.P.'s motives. I'm sending the information to your handheld right now. Let me know when the data arrives."

"Er...I can't do that right now, sir. I'm a bit busy gripping a tree trunk."

"Well, climb down, then."

Pockets shifts his weight to balance better. A leaf lands on Luna's nose, and she cranes her neck to see where it came from. She sniffs at the air, then loses interest and stops to scratch an itch with her hind leg.

"That might be a while," Pockets says, sending more leaves fluttering down as his tail twitches crazily.

"Why?" his father asks. Then his words speed up. "Are you in danger?"

"Yes," Pockets replies.

"No," I reply at the same time.

"Explain," the chief demands.

"There is a huge dog at the base of the tree," Pockets says.

"It is a tiny dog," I argue. "Barely the size of a loaf of bread."

Pockets's dad is silent. All I hear is heavy breathing.

"Sir?" I ask. "Are you still there?"

Then, his voice quivering, Pockets's dad asks, "Does the beast have long, pointy teeth?"

"Yes," Pockets says hurriedly.

I glance down at Luna, who is currently licking my calf. "No, sir," I reply. "Her teeth are small and stubby, like kernels of corn. Trust me, Pockets has stood up to the biggest, baddest criminals in the universe and won. This little dog wouldn't hurt any—"

But the chief ignores me. "Pilarbing!" he shouts. "I want you to remain calm and don't let go of that tree! Archie, I need you to use all your ISF deputy skills to protect my firstborn, my only son, my pride and joy. Do I need to fly out there? I can be there by morning."

I sigh. "I got this, Chief. No worries." I bend down and scoop Luna under one arm. She licks my face. As I head out of the courtyard, I hear Pockets say, "Stay with me, Daddy."

"Always, son."

As Mr. Goldblatt would say, *"Oy vey!"*

Chapter Three:
Plants Versus Pockets

It took nearly an hour to convince Pockets to come down from the tree. I wound up missing baseball practice, which I think Pockets was actually glad about. He had promised to come with me, even though he said watching humans play baseball is worse than watching Aniwerps play roly-poly-poppy, whatever THAT is! Instead, I spent the afternoon yelling up into a tree. It was Penny's idea to leave a can of tuna fish open on the ground. She's pretty smart for a three-year-old. Pockets climbed right down, gobbled it up, and announced (once Penny left to play on the swings) that he was ready to get to work on solving the mystery. He would need privacy and access to plenty of food and water, and some soft music would be nice.

He has been shut inside my bedroom closet ever since, having turned it into his own mini ISF headquarters. He tossed all my stuff out of the closet and shoved in three different computers and two printers, one of which makes 3-D objects instead

of just printing out paper! Once he solves his mystery, I plan on asking if I can use the 3-D printer to make a LEGO piece to replace the foot missing from my LEGO dinosaur. Penny took the foot last month because it was purple. Personally, I think she ate it. But if it ever comes out the other end, I definitely don't want it back.

Every few hours Pockets pops his head out, rubs his eyes with the back of his paw, and ducks back in. Dad and I keep offering to help, but he turns us down. I think he's a little embarrassed about his freak-out over tiny, harmless Luna and wants to prove he can do this on his own. Finally, I tell him I'm going to bed.

The *click-clack* of paws pounding on a keyboard (not to mention the paper crumpling and the muttering) makes sleeping impossible.

"Any chance of stopping for the night?" I call out. "Running around the block a million times tires a kid out."

The closet door creaks open and Pockets appears. His eyes are red and his ears are droopy. "This isn't any fun for me, either," he says. "Between this case and that horrid beast, I've missed seven naps today."

I sit up in bed. "Can you just tell me what you're looking for in there?"

He leaps onto the bed. "Fine. An attempted robbery was reported at a greenhouse on Alpha 43. This greenhouse contains a collection of the rarest plants in the universe and is very well guarded. The thieves toppled all the plants and mixed them up, so no one knows exactly what they were after. The only good news is that one of the guards grabbed the plant from the thieves before their daring escape through the sewer system. So now the ISF knows what the plant looks like, but not its name."

"Why would someone want to steal a plant?" Honestly, I'd hoped the mission would have been more exciting. A stolen plant that wasn't even really stolen? BORING!

Pockets yawns. "Many reasons, I suppose. You can make medicines out of some plants. Or maybe it has pretty flowers and they simply want it for their own garden. Perhaps they want to collect or sell it because it is rare. When an object is the only one of its kind, its value grows."

I think for a minute. "If they knew chances were good that they'd get caught, they must have wanted that one plant pretty bad."

"Exactly," Pockets says. "That's why the ISF is worried. If a group like B.U.R.P. is willing to take a big risk for something that seems to offer a very small reward, we must not be seeing the whole picture. I've been trying to find some information about the plant, but no luck so far. I'm also monitoring all the local police reports to see if any other plants have been reported stolen recently." Pockets yawns. "Maybe just a short nap." He curls his tail around his body, and before I can even lie down again, he's purring loudly, probably dreaming of mice swimming in a bowl of tuna fish.

Beep! Beep! Beep! Pockets and I bolt upright. The room is still dark, and Dad is not working tonight. So why is my alarm going off?

Pockets springs off the bed and into the closet. It takes me a few seconds to realize it's not my alarm going off at all. It's his computer.

He returns with a sheet of paper and holds it up, triumphant. "Got it! And we can cross off the idea that someone is after the plant because it's pretty."

He flicks his paw, but instead of his claws coming out, a little beam of light shines onto the page. That's a neat trick! The picture shows a small patch of yellow-brown weeds, like straw almost, but thicker, and droopy. Under the picture are these words:

Canisantha, NE, C-NP, D-TBD

"What do all those letters mean?" I ask.

"*NE* stands for *nearly extinct*," he says. "*Extinct* means when a type of plant or animal is no longer around anymore."

I roll my eyes. "I know what *extinct* means."

"How do I know what they teach in third grade on your planet?"

"Just go on."

"*C-NP* means *contact not poisonous*," he says. "There are no oils on the leaves that would harm your skin, the way poison ivy and poison oak can. *D-TBD* means that the effects of digesting the plant are *to be determined*. Which really means tests haven't been done on it."

I glance down at the picture again. I sure wouldn't want to eat that. "All right, then," I say, snuggling under my blanket. "Case closed. See ya tomorrow."

"Not so fast. This morning we worked on some physical drills; now let's do some brain training. If we want to catch the people trying to steal canisantha, what should we do?"

I'm tempted to say *Just let them have*

it—it's only a plant, but I'm pretty sure that's not the correct answer. "I don't know," I tell him instead, which isn't much better. "It's extinct anyway, right?"

"It's only *nearly* extinct," he reminds me. "That means it exists somewhere, only in very tiny amounts. I'm going to research where to find canisantha in the wild. Then in the morning we'll saddle up the space taxi and wrangle us a couple of plant thieves."

"Why are you talking like a cowboy?" I mumble as I doze off. I hear him say something about watching movies about the Old West on TV with Dad, but that's all I remember until I hear a bloodcurdling *screeeeech!*

Once again, I bolt upright, my heart

pounding this time. More yowling and screeching. I jump out of bed. "Pockets?" I open the closet door, but he's not in there. "Pockets! Where are you?"

"Yooowl...eeeekkk...meeeooowww!"

I drop to the floor next to the bed and press my cheek to the rug. At first I can't see anything in the dark, but then Pockets's eyes glint and I spot him. At that moment, Mom, Dad, and Penny run into the room.

"What's going on?" Dad asks, flipping on the light switch. "Is everything all right?"

Penny is wrapped around Mom's leg, clutching her stuffed dragon and sucking her thumb. She still does that only when she's really scared.

"Everything's fine," I tell them. "I mean, Pockets is upset about something, but I don't know what. Maybe he had a bad dream?"

From beneath the bed, Pockets whimpers. Since Penny's in the room, he can't tell us anything. I notice something I wasn't able to see in the dark—a newly balled-up piece of paper just outside the closet door. The others set about trying to get Pockets to come out while I unfold the paper. It has only one sentence printed on it:

The last remaining canisantha plant in the universe grows on the highest peak of planet Canis.

I pull Dad aside and whisper, "I think this is where our next mission will be. But I don't know why Pockets is so freaked out."

Dad looks down at the paper. "I know why," he says. "*Canis* is the word scientists give to the group of animals that includes the common dog."

"So you're saying that *planet Canis* means...*dog planet*?"

Dad nods. "'Fraid so."

"*Oy vey!*" I exclaim.

Dad looks at the shaking Pockets and says, "You can say *that* again!"

CHAPTER FOUR:
No Way, No How

"Good morning, Minerva," Dad says into the com system as he adjusts his rearview mirror. "Morningstar and son checking in."

"Always nice to hear from you," Minerva says cheerily, "but I don't have you on the schedule for today."

"The ISF is sending us out on a mission," Dad replies. "I will plug in our destination now." He presses a button on the dash, and the keyboard pops out. But instead of typing in the data, he turns the keyboard in my direction.

"Here's the information, Archie," he says, handing me a slip of paper. "You should learn how to do this." Dad hasn't let me touch anything on the dashboard yet! I eagerly begin inputting the information.

Destination: planet Canis in the Canis Major dwarf galaxy

Takeoff: 8:00 a.m.

Arrival: approx. 1:00 p.m.

Time and date of return: unknown

Passengers: Salazar Morningstar, Archie Morningstar, Agent Pilarbing

Fangorious Catapolitus, aka Pockets
the cat

    Systems: checked and ready

    Weather: partly cloudy

I'm not the world's best typist, so it takes me a lot longer than it would have taken him.

"Good job," Dad says, pushing the keyboard back in. Pleased, I slide my space map out of its case so I'll be ready as soon as we get the all clear from Minerva. But when she does come back on the com line, she's laughing so hard she can't speak. And let me tell you, the sound of a mouse laughing isn't all that pleasant. It's high-pitched and whiny and hurts my ears. "There is no way you're telling me that cat is going to planet Canis," she finally says. "No way, no how."

I almost tell her that's exactly what Pockets said last night when Dad told him we would be leaving early in the morning, but I feel like I have to defend him. "He *is* going," I insist.

"Then where is he?" she asks.

"He's coming," I reply, glancing out the taxi's back window.

"You expect me to believe," she says, "that a cat is going to willingly travel to a planet inhabited by nothing but dogs? And I don't mean civilized dogs that walk and talk and have cities and play ball games. I mean wild dogs whose first thought when they see a cat is to chase it."

That news about the dogs being wild surprises me. I figured they were talking dogs, like Pockets is a talking cat

and Minerva is a talking mouse. "Well...
maybe not exactly *willingly*," I admit.

"Here he comes now!" Dad says. He
and I jump out of the car. Mom and Penny
are pushing Pockets in the crate that Dad
rigged together in the middle of the night.
It's like the world's largest cat carrier, but
on wheels. A regular-size cat could easily squeeze between the wooden slats, but
Pockets can only stick his paws through.

Pockets scowls at us when he's wheeled
up to the car. I know he has a lot he'd like
to say to my dad and me, but he can't say
anything in front of Penny. We only got
him into the crate in the first place because
he fell into such a deep sleep after all the
yowling and carrying-on. Dad and I were
able to slide him right in without waking

him. The motion of the crate kept him sleeping, so Mom and Penny have been rolling him up and down the block for the last hour like a baby in a stroller. Looks like he finally woke up!

"Got a lot of strange glances," Mom tells us. Penny kneels down beside the crate. Her cheeks get all puffy when she wants to say something but can't get the words out. We're used to it. Only this time, once she lets out the air, she breathes in again and says, "Bye-bye, Pockets. Please come home soon."

Mom, Dad, and I gasp. Even Pockets stops glaring at us, and his ears perk up. That is the longest sentence Penny has ever said. It may actually be the ONLY full sentence she's ever said. In fact, it was really TWO sentences! Mom's eyes fill with tears, and she bends down to pull Penny into her arms. "Oh, sweetie! I'm so proud of you! Talking like the big girl you are! And of course Pockets is coming back. Daddy's just taking him on a little ride."

Penny squirms out of Mom's arms and reaches through the slats into the crate. Pockets moves closer so she can stroke his neck. "I love you, Pockets!" she says. "You're the best pet ever!"

Of course this makes Mom fully start to cry. Dad and I may have wiped away a tear or two—I'm not gonna lie.

"We'd better get going," Dad says, patting Penny on the head. "Otherwise we'll never leave."

It takes me, Dad, *and* Mom to lift the crate into the backseat. It doesn't help that Penny and Pockets keep reaching for each other. Penny has begun listing all the ways that Pockets is the best pet—he's cute, he's cuddly, he sleeps on her bed and keeps her feet warm, his purrs sound like music, and on and on. I guess now that Penny has decided to start talking, she has no plans to ever stop!

As soon as the car door closes and Mom leads Penny away, Pockets starts yelling at us. "What do you think you're doing? I outrank you! I order you to release me and deliver me back to the apartment!"

"I knew it!" Minerva says, her laughter cackling through the com line.

"Hey," Pockets shouts at her. "I haven't seen you book a trip to MY planet!"

The idea of a mouse vacationing on a planet full of cats quiets her right down.

"Let's just focus on the job ahead," Dad

says, heading out of town toward the airfield. "We know you don't want to go, Pockets. And trust me—your father is beside himself with worry, but he knows you're the best officer for the job. He made us promise to keep you far away from any dogs. You'll stay with the taxi while Archie and I retrieve the plant."

Pockets finally settles down. "I don't have to leave the taxi?" he asks.

"That's right," Dad says.

"We can use those glasses and the earpiece you gave me yesterday," I suggest to Pockets. "That way it will be like you're there with us."

"Fine," he grumbles, pulling out his pillow. He curls up on top of it but doesn't shut his eyes.

"Ready for liftoff?" Dad asks me.

I turn back around and focus on the map. I ask it for the best route, and the map responds to my voice by filling the air over my lap with planets and stars.

"That's strange," I say, turning the map around to get a better view. "The Canis Major dwarf galaxy is right next to our Milky Way, but the trip to get there is really long and winding. And the travel time we sent Minerva said five hours. We've passed through *ten* galaxies before in less time than that."

"Yes, but there aren't any wormholes between us and Canis Major," Dad says, raising his voice over the increasing roar of the engine and the grinding sound the wings make as they come out from the sides of the taxi. "That means we can't take any shortcuts. You'll have to pay careful attention because we'll be passing through a lot of populated areas. There will be many more stars and planets than you're used to navigating around."

That sounds scary! I make sure my double seat-belt system is tight and brace myself as the front wheels lift off the ground. That first part—when half the car is flying and half is driving—still takes some getting used to.

I focus on my space map. There are so many objects floating in front of me that I can barely see the dashboard through them. "Okay," I reply, peering at it all nervously. "We'll have to exit the solar system after we pass Mars. There are a lot of asteroids flying between the orbits of Mars and Jupiter, though."

"Yup," Dad says, slowing as we approach Mars. "That's the Asteroid Belt. We can usually avoid flying through it, but sometimes the only way around is through."

I reach out with my finger and touch one of the tiny map asteroids whizzing by my face in an almost perfect circle. It's moving so fast that the words above it are hard to read. I think they're telling me the rock is one of millions zooming around this part of the solar system. Now all I have to do is make sure we avoid them all!

"Hang on, guys," I tell Dad and Pockets. "It's gonna be a bumpy ride!"

CHAPTER FiVE:
What Would Pockets Do?

For a half hour I shout out directions like: "Turn east! No, not yet...now! Okay, straight past the asteroid that looks like a giant football. Okay, slow down so the one that looks like Pockets's butt can pass in front of us. I don't want that thing getting too close!"

Pockets *harumph*s from the backseat, but Dad laughs. I think he's having fun zigging and zagging to avoid the giant rocks. My stomach's getting a little queasy, but we're almost out of the Asteroid Belt. At least there were no loop-the-loops like in the wormholes.

The rest of the trip to Canis is long, but we get to see some really cool things on the way. Right as we leave the Milky Way, Dad points out a stellar nursery where stars are starting to form. A special coating on the windshield allows us to actually see the gas and dust swirling around us, clumping together to form baby stars. I point it out to Pockets, but he only grunts at me. I don't take it personally.

"We are about to enter the atmosphere for Canis," I finally announce. Pockets springs up, hits the top of his crate, yelps, and shouts something that makes my dad say, "Young man, we don't use that kind of language in this taxi!"

"Sorry," Pockets mutters miserably. Then he swings his tail around, unhinges the end, and lasers a hole right through the side of the crate. He walks out onto the seat and stretches. "Ah, that's better," he says.

"Why didn't you just do that from the start?" I ask.

He shrugs. "What would be the point? I knew I needed to come with you. So guide us to the right mountaintop, oh keeper of the space map. Let's grab the plant before B.U.R.P. does, and then get out of Dodge."

"Dodge?" I ask, searching my map. "I don't see any planets with that name."

Dad chuckles. "It's not a planet. It's an expression from old western movies. It means 'to leave town quickly.'"

I feel a little left out of their late-night movie marathons, but truthfully, those old black-and-white movies are kinda boring. "Well, anyway, as soon as we pass that mountain over there with the snow on it, you'll see a peak with two tall trees. According to the ISF, that's where the plant grows."

Dad follows my instructions, but as soon as we approach the peak with the two trees, we all see the problem. There's nowhere to land! The whole mountaintop, including the trees, is about the size of our kitchen!

"Archie, you're going to have to go down there while the taxi hovers overhead," Pockets says. "I, of course, will remain here." He pulls out a folded ladder and begins unrolling it. "For added protection, you can use my force field device. As they taught us at the academy, if you fall, you'll bounce back up like a rubber ball."

"Seriously?" I ask. Pockets is always serious, so I turn to Dad. "You're going to let me climb out the window, in midair, and climb down this ladder?"

Dad takes a closer look out the window. "I can hover right next to that smaller tree. You won't actually be too far off the ground, so I'm okay with it if you are."

My eyes widen. "Awesome!"

While Dad gets into position, Pockets

414

rolls down the back window and attaches the ladder. It unfolds until the last rung dangles only a foot off the ground. "We'll get you as close as we can to the plant," he says, "so you won't have to get off the ladder. I think it's best not to step on the ground so the dogs don't pick up your scent as quickly."

I'd kind of forgotten about the dogs.

He hands me his force field pen and shows me what button to press to turn it on and off. "You'll have to enclose the whole taxi and the ladder, too," he says. "Otherwise you won't be able to grip the rope. Making such a wide field will quickly drain the battery, though, so make sure you turn it off when you land."

I nod, slipping the gadget into my back pocket.

"One more thing," Pockets says, pulling out a small pouch with a metal clip at the end. He clips it onto my belt loop and then sprays it all over with Camo-It-Now. "This will keep the plant safe and hidden."

"Cool," I say, reaching down to touch the now-invisible pouch. Yup, still there. Then I slide my space map into its silver case and sling it over my shoulder. After wishing I'd had it with me on the last planet to help me rescue a three-eyed princess, I'm never leaving it behind again!

"Ready?" Pockets asks.

"Giddyap!" I reply. It's the only cowboy phrase I know.

Dad gives me the thumbs-up and says, "Might not want to tell your mom about this one for a little while."

I grin and climb over my seat into the back. Pockets helps me get out the window and onto the top rung of the ladder. Once I have a solid grip, I activate the force field. I wave good-bye and begin the climb down. The ladder sways more than I'd like, but knowing that the force field is around me makes me feel braver. I look up at the car to see Pockets sticking his head out the window, watching. I can tell from his face that he wishes he could do this, too. That cat loves adventure.

When I reach the last rung, I undo the force field and look around. From my perch on the bottom rung, I can see a single stalk of the canisantha plant growing in a shady spot between the two trees, just out of my reach. If I tried to grab it and fell, would the dogs pounce on me? I wave up to Dad

and Pockets to tell them they need to move the taxi a few feet, but they just think I'm waving to say hello and so they wave back. Not helpful.

I swing for a few seconds and ask myself, *What would Pockets do?* He would do the best with what he had. Although in his case, with his endlessly deep pockets, he has everything! So I use what I have. I untie each end of the strap from my map case, then tie one end onto the rung of the ladder above me and the other end onto my belt loop. Now when I lean forward, I can let go of the ladder just enough to grab the plant without my hands or feet touching the ground. The plant feels rough, like bark, rather than soft like leaves. I can definitely see why no one wanted to try eating it!

Pockets told me to pull it out with the roots still attached, so I grab the stalk with both hands and tug. It doesn't budge. I yank harder and harder until it finally comes away in my hands. If I didn't know better, I would think the ground knew it was holding on to something so valuable and rare. I fumble for the invisible pouch and place the plant carefully inside it. As it drops back against my pants pocket, I remember I'd put the glasses and earpiece from Pockets in there. D'oh! I could have used those before! I put them on now and instantly hear Pockets shouting in my ear, "Get off the ladder! Let go of the rope! Hide behind the closest tree! Now!"

I don't even have time to think or ask

Why? or *What about the dogs?* I quickly untangle myself from the strap and dash toward the tree. The second I step away from the ladder, it shoots up and the taxi zooms off behind a nearby cloud.

So now I'm on the ground and the dogs could come at any second and there's nowhere to go. Pockets was right—I should have brushed up on my tree climbing!

"Hurry!" Pockets shouts. But I'm not moving fast enough. I know this because a very large, very hairy hand that definitely doesn't belong to Pockets or Dad—or, fortunately, a wild dog!—has just clamped down on my shoulder.

Chapter Six:
A Case of Mistaken Identity

I stand very still, afraid to turn and face the guy beside me. I'm thinking that maybe the dogs wouldn't have been so bad after all. I mean, dogs like me. At least Luna does. Maybe they would have wanted to play fetch or find a nice river to splash in.

Instead, I get *this* huge guy. (I can tell he's huge by the shadow he casts. He reminds me of Mr. Fitch, the first criminal I ever helped catch.)

"Stay calm, Archie," Pockets says in my ear. "If you can, switch on the glasses so I can see what you're seeing."

As soon as I make a move to lift my arm, the guy spins me around to face him. He is dressed in tight-fitting black clothes with a badge sewn onto the sleeve that says B.U.R.P. When he sees my face, his overly large green eyes (with no eyelids that I can spot!) widen in surprise. He quickly lets go of me and backs away. "Forgive me," he says. "I thought you were back at the spaceship napping after working so late last night. If you don't mind my asking, why are you wearing those strange clothes?"

"Er...um...huh?" I am not proud of them, but these are the only words I can come up with. I take this moment of confusion to turn on the glasses, though. The lenses flicker, and I know Pockets can see what I'm seeing now.

"He's a high-ranking B.U.R.P. agent!" Pockets says into my earpiece. "A big shot in the organization. He must think you are one of the other leaders' kids! Don't correct him."

"We should get you back up there," the man says. "We have the big meeting soon." He looks around. "How about I grab the plant now and be done with it? We don't really need to wait for the scientists to come down here."

He steps toward the trees. Uh-oh!

"Tell him to wait!" Pockets shouts in my

ear. "Tell him the plant is very fragile and you need an expert to handle it correctly! He can't find out that you have it already!"

I try to sound very commanding as I relay Pockets's commands. The B.U.R.P. agent grumbles a bit but steps back.

"Okay, then," I say. "Gotta go. See ya." I turn away, but he reaches out to stop me.

"I know you like your fresh air," he says, "but we must stay on schedule." He taps his watch. "Plus, you know it isn't safe out here with all the wild dogs."

It's weird that he doesn't blink.

"Archie, it's Dad," my father's voice says in my ear. "Pockets gave me an earpiece, too. He says this could be our only chance to get on a B.U.R.P. spaceship and learn their plans. You can use the force field, and

426

of course we can be on board in less than a minute if you need us. Pockets already sprayed Camo-It-Now on the taxi and jammed B.U.R.P.'s radar so they won't know we're here." He lowers his voice and says, "Archie, this is a big deal, and if you're not ready for it, just say so. Honestly, I'm not ready for it, but I'm trying to be brave for the both of us."

I sort of want to cry, but I also really want to see inside a spaceship. I take a deep breath. "I'm ready."

The agent nods, assuming I'm speaking to him. He leads me toward a circle of white chalk a few feet away from us. The pouch with the plant in it bounces against my leg. I hope the Camo-It-Now doesn't wear off!

"After you," he says, motioning for me to step inside the circle. This seems like a very odd thing to do. Is a net going to spring up from the ground and trap me? I risk a quick glance up at the sky. I don't see the B.U.R.P. ship. Just a few puffy clouds. Maybe it's invisible, like the taxi.

"Go on," Pockets urges in my ear. Then, as though he knew what I'd been thinking, he adds, "It will be fine. I promise. Their ship is cloaked, too. No doubt for a quick mission like this, they only brought a small one. You'll look around for a few minutes, and then we'll come get you."

The agent gives me a gentle nudge toward the circle. The nudge, combined with the fact that I can now see a large pack of enormous black-and-gray dogs circling the base of the mountain, is enough to land me in the circle. The second both feet are inside, I feel a tingling that spreads up my body. For a moment I'm worried that whatever they're doing to me, it's going to cause my feet to stick to the ground, and those dogs seem like good climbers! They look more like wolves than dogs—not that a city kid like me has ever seen a real wolf. Still, they definitely don't look like they want to play fetch.

But it turns out that they are NOT trying to stick my feet to the ground. In fact, it's more like the exact opposite. With a *whoosh*, my feet lift off the ground, and I'm zooming up into the sky, right toward the largest, puffiest cloud! My hair whips around my head, and I quickly grab for my space map so it doesn't fly away. I hope that pouch is clipped on tight! I look down. The agent is zooming up below me. He looks bored, as though he does this every day.

I'm about to tell Pockets to rescue me RIGHT NOW and forget about the plan, when I suddenly shoot into the cloud. I'M IN A *CLOUD*! It is pretty much what you'd expect a cloud to be like—cold and wet and white. I tilt my head back and look up, which may have been a mistake, because now I know I'm heading right toward a huge metal object with B.U.R.P. 01 painted across the bottom. All I can think to do is fling my arms over my head.

A few seconds later, a round hole appears in the bottom of the ship and I'm sucked inside. The floor instantly seals

beneath me. Going from zooming to standing throws me off balance, and I stumble backward, trying to catch my breath.

It's a good thing I moved, because the hole in the floor is back! The agent appears beside me—or, I should say, his *head* appears. The rest of him follows quickly behind. The floor closes up beneath him. He pats down his hair and adjusts his shirt.

"Well, that was something!" Dad's awed voice comes through my earpiece. "Pockets lent me the glasses. I felt like I was right there with you in that cloud! Gotta get me a pair of those!"

Now that I'm not terrified anymore, I realize it really WAS pretty cool!

"Come," the agent says. "You need to get back to your rooms. You can't very well show up to the meeting wearing *that*."

I'm a little insulted on behalf of my clothes, but I let his comment go.

The agent leads me through a series of long, narrow hallways lined with doors on one side and windows on the other. The windows show mostly a view of the cloud that hides the ship, but every once in a while I catch a glimpse of the sky and the mountainside. Pockets must have been wrong—this isn't a small ship. It's huge!

I don't see the taxi anywhere, which I know is how it's supposed to be. Then I remember I CAN see it. Well, the inside of it, at least! I can use the glasses! The agent has begun talking into a communication device on his wrist, so I slow down to widen the gap between us, then flick the switch.

And suddenly it's like I'm right there!

Pockets must have taken the glasses back, because I can see Dad in the driver's seat, tapping his fingers anxiously on the steering wheel. I want to shout, but I force myself to whisper. "Dad! I can see you!"

Dad jolts upright, his hand reaching for his earpiece. "Hey, Archie!" He reaches over to Pockets, and I can tell he's ruffling the fur on top of his head. I try not to laugh. Dad always used to ruffle my hair when I was little. Okay, sometimes he still does.

"Hey," Pockets grumbles. "Ask next time!"

Dad ignores him. "Son, I'm very proud of you. You're being very brave."

"Thanks, Dad," I whisper.

"We'll be right here with you," he says.

Then Pockets chimes in with, "Try to

explore as much of the ship as you can. I'm recording what you're seeing through your lenses."

I'm about to suggest hiding instead of exploring, when Pockets adds, "You'd better switch back now."

Dad gives a wave and I reluctantly turn the view back to the ship. It's a good thing I didn't wait much longer, because the agent has just stopped in front of a large wooden door and is waiting for me to catch up.

The door is much fancier than any we've passed so far. I don't see a doorknob or key-hole anywhere, though. The agent presses a nearly invisible button beside the door, and a keypad appears. He steps aside and gestures for me to use it. I look back at him blankly. He shakes his head. "Forgive me, but you'd forget your own birthday if it wasn't written down on one of those lists of yours," he says, punching in a series of numbers. The door slides into the wall with a nearly silent *swoosh*. "I will see you down in the laboratory in twenty minutes," he says, then turns and strides back in the direction we came from.

I stand in the hallway for a minute, not sure if I should go in or stay here. Voices headed my way from the end of the hallway make my decision for me. I jump into the room. The door *swoosh*es closed behind me, plunging me into total darkness.

Why did I agree to this again?

Chapter Seven:
On Board the Mother Ship

I feel around the wall until I find a switch, but I don't turn the light on yet. What if the person whose room I'm in is waiting to jump out at me? Or the agent was tricking me and I'm actually in a jail cell? "Anytime now," Pockets nudges through the earpiece. Boy, he sure can be bossy, even long-distance!

I take a deep breath and flick the switch. The room lights up, and it's hands down the fanciest room I've ever seen outside of the movies or a magazine. Like five-star-hotel fancy. Like millionaire-movie-star fancy, with thick white carpets and gold statues and colorful paintings and shiny marble floors and tall columns with flowers and fruit bowls and glass cases filled with stuff I can't even identify from here. This one room is bigger than our whole apartment. Whoever that guard thinks my parents are, they must be very powerful and important people.

"Wow," Pockets says with a whistle.

"I know!" I reply. I rest my space map by

the door and take a few steps into the main part of the room. Up close, I can see that each glass case is filled with something weirder than the next. One has a sign with the words: THE LAST BOOGLER FISH. A large bowl of water sits inside the case. Swimming around the bowl is a tiny purple fish with long, floppy, bunny-like ears. I didn't even know fish *had* ears. "Hmm," Pockets says. "The boogler fish has been considered extinct for five years."

I move on to the next case. This one contains only a thin silver vase with a pink-and-white-striped flower sticking out. The sign reads: THE LAST LILANDRA FLOWER. A quick glance at the other cases tells me that each item—a leather-bound book, a metal coin, an animal horn—is the last of its kind.

THE LAST BOOGLER FISH

"I guess we know why B.U.R.P. wanted the plant," I tell Pockets. "Whoever lives here definitely likes to collect rare things."

"That's actually a relief," Pockets says. "Now at least we know B.U.R.P. wasn't after the plant as part of some sinister plot they were cooking up."

"Good! Then can you guys come pick me up now?"

"Soon," Pockets says. "You don't appear

to be in any danger, so would you mind taking a closer look around? See if you can find anything with the collector's name on it."

"Fine," I grumble. "But after this I want a raise."

"You're not even getting paid," Pockets points out.

"Then how about when I get back, you'll agree to come watch me play baseball?"

"Deal," he says. "Now go snoop around his desk. Try to find that list the agent mentioned."

I head toward a wide wooden desk piled high with papers. I spot a few computers and some gadgets that look a lot like ones I've seen Pockets use. "Hey," I say, picking up a force field pen. It says PROPERTY OF THE

ISF down the side! I pat my back pocket. Mine's still there.

"I knew it!" Pockets says. "B.U.R.P.'s been stealing our technology! That's how they always manage to stay one step ahead of us!"

I lift up the top sheet of paper and am about to peek at it, when I hear a low, wheezy sort of rumble. I freeze. It's quiet for few seconds, then I hear it again. It almost sounds like...

"Snoring!" Pockets, Dad, and I exclaim at the same time. I turn away from the desk, shoving the piece of paper into my pocket.

Behind me is the outline of a door. It blends into the wall so well I wouldn't have spotted it if not for the snoring coming from behind it. I tiptoe past the door, but I must have stepped too close, because it *whoosh*es open! Hasn't B.U.R.P. heard of *doorknobs*?!

The only light in the room is coming from glowing numbers projected on the wall, but I can still make out a few things. The huge bed in the center of the room is hard to miss, as is the boy-shaped lump under the blanket. At the bottom of the bed lies a small black cat. The boy-shaped lump is gently snoring. The cat-shaped lump is staring at me suspiciously with his greenish-gold cat eyes.

In my ear Pockets says, "Can you walk closer to the wall? I think it's a clock. I want to see how much time we have until he wakes up for the meeting at the laboratory."

"I'd really rather not," I whisper back. The cat is now sitting up, tilting his head at me. Something about the way he moves is familiar, but I don't have time to think about that now. The son of a clearly very important B.U.R.P. agent is about to wake up!

Two things happen at once. The cat lets out a loud meow right in my face as the numbers on the wall begin counting down: 59...58...57...56...

Something's going to happen in less than a minute! I'm pretty sure I don't want to be here when it does!

"We have to get to that meeting before he does!" Pockets says.

I'm more concerned with getting out of the room before he wakes up. I turn to run, but the cat springs up off the bed and jumps right at me!

I scramble backward and wind up directly at the foot of the bed. A beam of light suddenly shoots out from the wall and sweeps across my face. "Alarm off," a mechanical voice says.

The numbers on the wall disappear.

Oops! Someone is going to miss his meeting!

I run out of the room without looking back. Unfortunately, the cat has followed me out. I bend down to usher him back into the room before the boy wakes up and finds his cat gone. The cat won't budge. He just sits there, purring at me. I pick him up and move away from the door, which finally *whoosh*es closed behind me.

"Is that...?" Pockets begins. "It can't be.... Is it?"

I squint at the cat. He really DOES seem familiar. At the sound of Pockets's voice in my earpiece, the cat squirms his way up my arm and nuzzles my ear! I gasp. "Pockets! This is the cat from the castle on Tri-Dark! The one who followed you around the castle on our last mission!"

"Yes, I believe it is," Pockets says. "And that means the boy in the bed is the same one who escaped from us!"

"You'd better not come on the ship or you might wind up his pet again!"

"Very funny," Pockets says.

The last time Pockets and I had seen this cat was in a castle on a planet far away from here. A boy whose face was hidden by the hood of his black cloak was feeding

446

him and a bunch of other cats. The boy had taken a liking to Pockets, but Pockets was able to escape. I guess this other cat decided to stick around.

"What's important right now is that we get to that meeting," Pockets says. "We have to find the laboratory."

I grab my space map from where I'd left it by the front door. I pull it out of the tube and unroll it on the floor.

As I'd hoped, the whole floor plan of the B.U.R.P. ship rises into the air above my map. The ship is much bigger that I would have suspected, filled with rooms labeled with big words like CAFETERIA, MEDICAL BAY, LABORATORY, CONTROL ROOM, DOCKING BAY, RESEARCH AND DEVELOPMENT, and WEAPONS STORAGE, and many labeled PRIVATE, KEEP OUT.

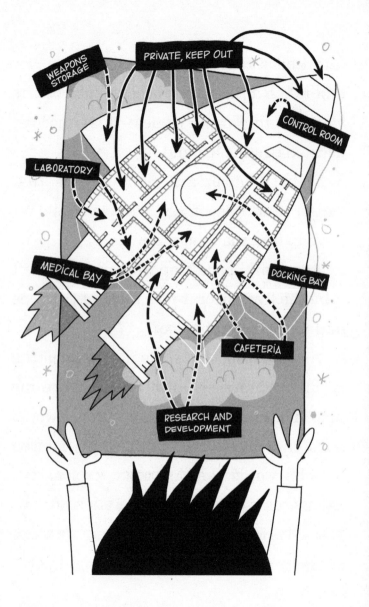

Pockets gasps. "Archie! This isn't just any B.U.R.P. ship you're on. This is the *mother ship*! The head of their whole fleet! Only the mother ship would have all those rooms!"

I try not to think of what any of that means and instead focus on finding the laboratory. "This is where I have to go," I tell Pockets, pointing to a room two flights down.

"Hurry," Pockets says. "The meeting is about to start. Whatever it's about is obviously important."

I quickly shove my map back into the case and at the last second remember I spotted a closet while searching for the light switch earlier. I rush over and root through the coats until I find what I'm looking for.

First, I tie the black cloak around my shoulders. Then I flip the hood up so it hangs over my face the same way the boy wore it when we spotted him on Tri-Dark.

I turn to face the full-length mirror inside the closet. "How do I look?" I ask Pockets.

"Like a fake vampire about to go trick-or-treating," he replies.

I peek out from under the hood. Hmm, he may be right. Still, just because that one B.U.R.P. agent might think all little boys look alike, it'll be safer to cover up. I don't know what happens to spies on the B.U.R.P. mother ship, and I don't want to find out.

CHAPTER EIGHT:
Woof!

With the help of my space map and my vampire costume, I make it to the meeting without anyone stopping me. It might be my imagination, but whenever one of the crew passes by, it almost feels like they're bowing their heads at me. Then they rush off without making eye contact. It must be the cape. I'm pretty sure at home it wouldn't get the same reaction! People would think I was trying to be a super-hero. Guess all planets are different!

The laboratory looks like a more high-tech version of the science class in my elementary school, with tall tables and beakers and Bunsen burners. This one also has lots of computer equipment, cameras, lasers, and aliens. The B.U.R.P. aliens look mostly human, but with slight differences—larger eyes and heads, wider shoulders, and a little more hair than you'd normally see on arms and legs. But no one has three eyes or purple skin or scales or feathers, so I blend in well enough...for about five seconds, that is. That's when every single person in the room turns to face me. I cringe while I wait for them to ask who I am and what I'm doing here, but no one does. Instead, a woman with long red hair and a white lab coat steps forward. A label on her coat reads HEAD SCIENTIST, B.U.R.P.

"Sir," she says, "the team we sent to the surface to gather the canisantha will return in a moment. I will add it to the mixture and we can begin the experiment." She pauses, then asks, "Where is the black cat?"

The cat? I clear my throat. "Um... taking a nap? Or... washing his paws? He does that a lot."

The scientist sighs. "Sebastian, I know how much you like cats. But we need to test the potion. Once all the ISF agents on Friskopolus have been turned into wild dogs, they will finally leave us alone. We will be able to rule the universe without them constantly ruining our plans."

I hear Pockets shouting in my ear, but I can't make sense of what he is saying, because I'm trying to make sense of what *she's* saying. First off, she thinks I'm someone named Sebastian; second... they want to turn ISF agents into *dogs*? We were definitely wrong to assume this Sebastian person just wanted the plant for his collection of rare or extinct things.

On the other end of the earpiece, Pockets is still freaking out. Dad cuts in and says, "Pockets and I are on the way. Distract them until we arrive."

Great. How am I supposed to do that?

Turns out I don't have to do anything, because just then the real Sebastian walks into the room. He looks almost exactly like me. Or I look almost exactly like HIM. His head is a little bigger, and his arms are hairier and his nose is kind of off center, but other than that, we could be twins. He is holding the little black cat under one arm.

"I'm sorry I'm late," Sebastian says to the scientist. "I was certain I had set my alarm clock, but it never went off. Did I miss anything? Do you have the plant?" He waits for the woman to answer, and when she only stares back, Sebastian finally notices everyone else has gone silent, too. "What's going on?" he asks.

The head scientist points a shaky finger at me. Sebastian follows the finger, and his eyebrows shoot up. "Who are *you*?" he asks, stepping forward. Before I can react, he pulls off my sunglasses and pushes my hood back to fully reveal my face. My hair springs up. Sebastian gasps and drops the black cat.

"You...you look just like me!" he says.

Actually, I'm at least an inch taller, but I think it's best not to mention this.

He reaches his hand toward my face, and for a second I think he's going to hit me! But instead he just pinches my cheek to make sure I'm real. "You may have my face," he says, "but you cannot possibly be the equal of Sebastian the Great, the universe's most feared criminal mastermind, not to mention the founder and leader of B.U.R.P. So who *are* you?"

Sebastian the Great? That's the best nickname he could come up with?

Wait! Did he just say he's the *leader* of B.U.R.P.? But he's just a kid!

He is waiting for an answer, so I say, "Um, big criminal mastermind here, too. You know, trying to rule the universe and all."

Sebastian walks around me in a full circle, glaring. I cringe as he steps right on my sunglasses, snapping them in half. "There is only room for one of us," he says, hands on his hips. "What is the name of your organization?"

"Um, it's F.A.R.T.," I blurt out, then instantly wish I could take it back. It was all I could think of!

The boy frowns. "What does it stand for?"

"That is top secret information," I tell him in my best evil-mastermind voice. Clearly, I have no idea what it might stand for.

He nods in grudging approval. "Only a few know what B.U.R.P. stands for, and they are sworn to secrecy. Now, I demand you tell me what you are doing on my spaceship. It certainly looks like you are pretending to be me!"

Pockets whispers in my ear, "Stay calm. We're almost there."

I begin to explain that this is all a misunderstanding, when the door bursts open. Relief floods through me. Pockets and Dad have arrived!

458

Only it isn't Pockets and Dad. It's another scientist in a white lab coat— a man this time, with white hair and a cane made of gleaming black wood. He is followed by the agent who brought me to the ship. I shrink back a little, but the agent walks right past me.

"The canisantha is missing!" the new scientist tells Sebastian. "The plant was there this morning. Our team confirmed it with long-range photography. See?" He holds up a photograph that shows the plant I took. I don't dare glance down at my pouch.

"Are you certain you looked in the right spot?" Sebastian asks.

"Yes," he replies. "Absolutely."

"The dogs must have gotten to it,"

Sebastian says. "You promised me that the plant was secure up there."

"It was," the scientist insists. "The slope is too steep for the dogs to climb. That's why it had remained safe all these years. Plus, the plant was pulled up by the roots. So whatever—or whoever—took it must have known the roots were important."

"But no one left the ship," Sebastian says.

The agent steps forward. "Well, no one but you, sir," he says, almost apologetically. "You know, earlier. When you were wearing those odd clothes."

"You are mistaken," Sebastian says. "I've been taking a nap!"

The agent looks torn between wanting to argue and not wanting to accuse his boss of lying. He looks down at his feet. I slowly try to back up into the crowd. This would be a good time to disappear.

But it's too late. The agent looks up and spots me. He takes in my outfit and realizes I'm the one he saw, not Sebastian. He looks back and forth between the two of us, then cries out, "What? Who? Huh?" In an awkward attempt to reach for me, he crashes into a vat of bright pink liquid that the crowd was blocking before. The head scientist grabs it before it topples.

"Almost there," Pockets whispers in my ear.

Sure, I've heard *that* before.

The agent turns to Sebastian. "Is this some kind of trick? Is this a brother of yours?"

The B.U.R.P. leader shakes his head. "I assure you, I have never seen this boy before in my life."

The agent thrusts his finger in my face. "You were standing right by those plants! *You* took it and tricked me! Where is it?"

Before I can even think, the white-haired scientist begins waving his cane in a wide circle right in front of me. To my horror, my secret pouch with the missing plant is suddenly no longer so secret. They know how to dissolve Camo-It-Now! I quickly pull the cloak around me, but it's too late. I know they've seen it.

"Get out of there now!" Pockets shouts in my ear. I know he can't see me, since my glasses are broken on the floor, but what he can hear in the earpiece obviously has him worried. I wish we'd gotten to the martial arts part of our training, because bouncing a ball and skipping rope isn't going to help me right now. Before I can make a move, the agent grabs me by both arms.

Sebastian reaches into my pocket and pulls out the bag. His eyes light up. "We've got it!" he shouts. He hands it to the woman, who pulls the plant out of the bag and drops it into the vat. The plant sizzles, then sinks to the bottom. The mixture begins to darken. The other scientist scoops up the small black cat, who meows in protest.

"Is there no other way to test if the potion will work on talking cats?" Sebastian asks.

The head scientist shakes her head.

"We need to test it on a regular cat first. Then we will know the proper amount to feed our real target. Don't worry. It will be very painless, and it will last forever." She dips a pair of tongs into the vat and pulls off a piece of the plant no bigger than a pea. She reaches toward the cat's mouth.

"Not so fast," a familiar voice shouts.

It's Pockets! Dad is right behind him. Finally!

"Hey, I know you!" Sebastian shouts back. "You're that giant cat from the castle at Tri-Dark! But...you're talking! How is that...?"

Pockets whips out his ISF badge. "You are under arrest for stealing the last canisantha plant and planning evil deeds."

At the sound of Pockets's voice, the

little black cat's ears perk up. He tries to wriggle out of the scientist's arms, but for an old guy, the man is very strong.

The woman is now only a few inches from the little cat's mouth. Without taking time to think, I reach into my pocket and grab the force field pen. I aim it so that an invisible wall shoots up between the cat and the woman. She bumps right into it and snarls.

Sebastian calmly walks toward the wall and taps on it with his ring. The wall disappears. "Did you really think you could use one of your ISF gadgets on my ship and succeed?"

I swallow hard.

Sebastian plucks the pea-size ball from the woman's hand and walks right up to

Pockets. "We were going to test this on a wild cat first, but you would make a much better test subject."

I expect Pockets to go screaming from the room, but he holds his ground.

"Or..." Sebastian continues, "what if you come work for us instead? We could use a giant cat like you around."

Pockets shakes his head. "Trust me—I don't make a very good pet."

I don't want Pockets to stay here, of course, but I don't want him to eat that plant, either. "You make a great pet," I argue. "Penny's only talking now because of you."

Sebastian doesn't take his eyes off Pockets. "What's it going to be?" he asks. "Life as a highly respected member of

B.U.R.P. or a lifetime as a dog, your natural-born enemy?"

"I'll take the dog," Pockets says calmly. Then he plucks the ball from Sebastian's hand and brings his paw up to his own mouth! My jaw falls open!

The scientist was right—the change DOES happen fast! One second I'm looking at a giant white cat, and then his head changes and his tail spreads out and he's a green dragon! Then a second later he's a squirrel! Then a turtle. Then he turns into a dog that looks a lot like little Luna from back home. And finally, with a loud howl, he becomes one of the wild dogs from the planet below. My heart sinks when I look at him, but the B.U.R.P. people are cheering and high-fiving.

Their celebration is short-lived. The door *swoosh*es open, and a swarm of agents wearing ISF badges burst into the room and spread out. None, I notice, are cats. The B.U.R.P. members begin to shout and run. The ISF agents arrest everyone they can catch. The dog who was once Pockets hops from foot to foot and barks like the regular dog he is. My heart aches for him, and for us.

Then I notice that the old-man scientist is about to grab the vat of liquid on the lab table. Dad and I look at each other and, with a nod, hurry over to the table. Dad gets there first and sweeps the vat off the table. "NO!" both scientists cry as it crashes to the ground. Once the liquid spills out, the plant dissolves until nothing is left.

"Come, Archie," Dad says, yanking me toward the door. "We've got to try to catch Sebastian. He ran out!"

"But we can't leave Pockets! We have to do something!"

"Pockets has it under control," Dad says, pulling me down the hall. "You need to trust him."

I hesitate for a second, listening to the barking and shouting in the room we just left. Poor Pockets! It doesn't seem as though he's in control at all. What are we going to tell Penny when Pockets doesn't come home with us? He's become a part of our family.

The only thing that makes me feel better is that the ISF is here now, so they will make sure Pockets is taken care of. He won't be left in B.U.R.P.'s hands.

We make it out of the room and into the empty hallway. One glance out the window tells us we're too late to capture Sebastian. Looming in front of us is an oddly shaped space shuttle. Sebastian is sitting at the helm, steering away from the mother ship.

"That's his suite of rooms!" I exclaim, recognizing the bed and the huge desk and the collection of rare objects. "It must detach from the ship!"

"Come," Dad says, grabbing my hand. "Maybe we can catch him in the taxi."

We run to the docking bay where Dad parked. I look into the empty backseat as I climb in, my eyes filling with the tears I managed to hold in until now. Then I blink. It looked like something on the seat had shimmered for a second. I hear a little buzz, like a fly, and blink again.

"Took you guys long enough," Pockets says, suddenly appearing in the seat, looking every inch his old self: white fur, gray pockets, fluffy ears, big belly.

I jump so high I hit my head on the roof of the car! "What? How? Huh?" I realize Sebastian said almost the exact same thing when he first saw me, but I don't care. I scramble over the seat and squeeze Pockets into a big hug.

"Okay, okay," he says, pushing me away, "that's enough."

"But how did you do it?" I ask, wiping my tears away. "The scientist said the change would last forever."

"And maybe it would have," Pockets

says, "if I had actually eaten the plant." He grins and opens his paw to reveal the tiny ball.

My eyes widen. "But...but I saw you turn into a dog! And some other crazy creatures before that!"

He shakes his head. "Remember how I used my Atomic Assembler device to temporarily turn you and your father into aliens on our last mission? Well, what you saw in the lab was me using the Atomic Assembler to temporarily turn myself into a dog. After you two left the room, I turned myself into a fly and zoomed out of there! By the time the scientists realize they've been tricked, they'll have been arrested by the ISF. Then they'll have bigger problems than worrying where the dog went."

"I'm sorry I couldn't tell you, Archie," Dad says. "But we didn't know who may have been listening, so Pockets made me promise to keep his plan a secret until we were all safely back in the taxi."

"I'm just glad you're you!" I hug Pockets one more time and then climb into my own seat. "Now let's go get Sebastian!"

But to my surprise, Pockets says, "Not today. I was tracking his ship while I waited for you. Once it left the orbit of planet Canis, it disappeared from my radar. B.U.R.P. has a lot of technology that we don't. We'll find him someday, but for now, capturing the mother ship was a huge turning point in our efforts to bring down B.U.R.P. and keep the universe safe. Let's head home to celebrate."

"Say no more," Dad says, revving the engine. I strap in and get my map ready. The sun is setting as we soar over the gold-and-green mountaintops.

"It's too bad we don't know what Sebastian's plotting next," Dad says as the planet disappears out our back window.

"Wait! That reminds me!" I reach into my front pocket and pull out the crumpled piece of paper I'd taken from Sebastian's desk before I even knew who he was. It has the words LONG-RANGE PLANS TO RULE THE UNIVERSE printed at the top. I hand the paper to Pockets and say, "Looks like you're not the only one with surprises in his pockets. I have a feeling this will keep the ISF busy for a long time."

Pockets reads the list and beams at

me. "You've definitely earned yourself that raise," he says. He reaches over the seat to pat me on the head with his heavy paw.

"Wait a second," Dad says. "Archie's getting *paid*?"

Pockets and I laugh. "You're still coming to my baseball game, right?" I ask Pockets.

"Wouldn't miss it," he says.

"Hey, Pockets," Dad says. "Now that you've been a dog, it's not so bad, right? I think we're going to get one as a pet."

In response, Pockets turns himself back into a fly and burrows into the corner of the seat.

This time Dad and I laugh at Pockets. "I was only kidding," Dad says.

I turn to look at my map. I have to

prepare to guide us back through the Asteroid Belt. Sure, Sebastian's still out there, but tonight my whole family will be together. I can't think of a better reason to celebrate than that.

Three Science Facts to Impress Your Friends and Teachers

1. GREENHOUSES are glass buildings used by botanists (scientists who study plants), professional gardeners, and backyard gardeners who may enjoy growing rare and exotic plants and flowers.

Sunlight passes through the glass walls of a greenhouse and is absorbed by the plants. The plants then give off their own heat, but that heat is unable to pass through the glass. This creates a warm environment and an even temperature in the greenhouse, allowing the plants to thrive. Greenhouses also protect plants from harsh elements like wind, rain, ice, and snow, and keep bugs and other animals away.

2. An animal or plant is considered EXTINCT when the last of the species is no longer alive. EXTINCTION happens for different reasons. Sometimes a particular animal is hunted too much, or a crop is overharvested. Sometimes forests are cut down, leaving animals without a home, or plants without the right environment to grow. Sometimes a new species is introduced into a habitat (a place where an animal or plant naturally lives or grows) and the existing animals can't compete.

Pollution in the air or water can also contribute to the extinction of a species. Thousands of animals and plants are on the ENDANGERED SPECIES LIST. This means there are so few of them left that it is illegal to harm them.

A MASS EXTINCTION happens when a large number of species become extinct at the same time. An asteroid caused the most recent mass-extinction event almost sixty-six million years ago. Three-quarters of all animal species, including all non-flying dinosaurs, became extinct.

3. An ASTEROID is a rock containing different types of metal. It orbits the sun, just as the planets do. But it is much, much smaller than a planet. In our solar system, the **ASTEROID BELT** orbits the sun between Mars and Jupiter. Scientists think it contains more than a million asteroids, ranging in size from a small pebble to a large country!

In the early days of our solar system, the planets were formed by gravity pulling dust and rocks together. Once Jupiter was formed, its strong gravity prevented a lot of those rocks from forming other planets; instead, the rocks were left to float around the sun. NASA currently has a spacecraft called DAWN exploring the largest asteroids in the Asteroid Belt in the hope of learning about life in the early formation of the solar system.

Whoever first discovers an asteroid gets to name it. Maybe one day an asteroid will be named after Archie or Pockets!

Don't miss the next SPACE TAXI adventure!

B.U.R.P. STRIKES BACK

Pockets is in a panic: All the tuna fish sandwiches on Akbar's Floating Rest Stop have been stolen! He thinks it's the fault of the irritating head of his alien fan club, but Archie suspects the mystery goes much deeper. Get ready for another thrilling and hilarious space adventure!

WENDY MASS has written lots of books for kids. MICHAEL BRAWER is a teacher who drives space taxis on the side. They live in New Jersey with their two kids and two cats, none of whom have left the solar system.